FEVER

WHERE SEX IS ALWAYS IN FASHION
BOOK THREE CLUB INFERNO

JAMIE K SCHMIDT

FREE BOOK

Thank you for picking up my book! I hope you enjoy it, and would consider leaving me a review.

If you'd like to keep up-to-date on my new releases and other fun things, please subscribe to my newsletter and get a *FREE BOOK*.

www.jkschmidt.com/newsletter

Be a VIP Reader and have a chance to win monthly prizes, free books and up-to-date information.

CHAPTER 1

Colleen Bryant's shoulder ached from the repeated use of the cane on Senator Clemmons's back. She was admiring her pattern and judging his pain level when he sighed and release shook through him.

"You didn't ask my permission," she said with a twinge of cold hatred.

"I'm sorry, Mistress."

She strode across the dungeon to put the cane away. Her boots clacked ominously on the lacquered floor. Picking up a leather quirt, Colleen strode back over to him and waited until he shut his eyes and whimpered.

"Count," she ordered, and whacked the small whip on his bare buttocks with a snap of her wrist.

He hissed an indrawn breath of pain and gritted out one through ten.

Colleen set her jaw, annoyed that his selfishness denied both of them the level of satisfaction they were striving for. If he didn't pay so well, and turned a blind eye in directions she didn't want anyone to look, she would have given him over to another Domme.

"Thank you, Mistress," he panted.

Normally, she'd soothe a vitamin A and E salve over her submissive's marks and fetch him a glass of cold water while he came down from the endorphin high. Today, she snapped her fingers and one of the other dungeon submissives scurried over to assist the senator.

"Thank you," Colleen heard him sigh again before she slammed the door.

Her hands, encased in black leather gloves, clenched into fists. She forced herself to relax one finger at a time. It wasn't as if she had been planning to orgasm during the session. Hell, the senator wanted just humiliation and someone to beat his ass, not an energetic sex scene. Still, there should be a connection between a Domme and sub—a trust that the senator would never give her. Colleen missed the feeling of being given the gift of absolute obedience.

But she'd gone in there knowing that Clemmons was a shitty sub. Now it was her turn to sigh. He was trying to learn the concept of letting go in order to achieve a more intense and satisfying orgasm. She'd thought that this time he'd trust her enough to take him the distance so he could fully immerse himself in submission. She shook her head. Not going to happen. The senator always rushed to orgasm, as if he was afraid it would be taken away from him. Biting her lip, Colleen wondered if she could get him to bring his wife to a session.

"All work and no play makes Colleen a dull girl." Dante uncoiled himself from the wall he had been leaning on and caught up to her in three easy strides. Colleen had walked right by him without even noticing he was there. She gave him a sneer over her shoulder. Speaking of men who needed some time in her dungeon . . .

Dante's green eyes were his most striking feature and he played it up with subtle dark eyeliner. His short black hair, neatly trimmed beard, and mustache gave him a Mephistophelian air. It didn't help the image that sometimes he stroked his mustache like a villain in the old black-and-white films.

"Don't you have something better to do than hang around outside my dungeon?" Colleen asked as she kept walking. She mentally called up the Doms' schedules and thought that he had an advanced breath play workshop about to start.

He stopped her with a gloved hand on her throbbing shoulder. She tried not to wince, but he was good enough to catch the slightest tremor.

"You should ice that," he said, all hints of teasing gone. "Then get into the hot tub and let the jets pound out some of that tightness."

Colleen turned around to face him as he let his hand drop. Blowing the blond wave out of her eye, she nodded. "If I get to it. Now, what did you want?"

"You. On your knees."

A flare of amusement danced through her, and she felt a real smile stretch across her face. It was an old game between the two of them, two Doms who didn't like to be topped trying to force the other one into a submissive position.

"You first," she countered. "And if I like what I see, I might allow you to lick my boots."

A hard flush started up Dante's collar, and his eyes narrowed. Colleen knew that he didn't like defiance, didn't like that she didn't tremble at his charisma. She deliberately stepped into his personal space and watched him check himself so he didn't take a step back. His nostrils flared and he stared at her mouth.

"You can't get to the next level as a Master if you don't experience the limits of your submission," he said.

"Thanks for mansplainin' that." Colleen rolled her eyes. While he was right that if you couldn't feel empathy for the sub you were a poor Dom, Colleen had a feeling Dante wasn't chasing her for altruistic reasons, so she could improve her craft. He was also assuming that she hadn't experienced being a submissive. What he knew about her training could fit in his mouth like a ball gag.

She had started her career as a sub, but it wasn't in her nature. She made more money on the other end of the whip and enjoyed it more. She had even married one of the most thrilling Doms she had ever met and gladly submitted to him. But after Alfie's death, she found comfort in giving the orders. None of that was Dante's business. Colleen earned her right to Domme the Doms in Club Inferno. It was her leadership that had grown Club Inferno, a secret BDSM club, into one of the hottest dungeons in the Northeast. And it was her bankroll that shielded them from unwanted inquiries by fronting a fashion resort called Couture, which was also one of the premier locations on the East Coast.

"What makes you think I need instruction from you?" She gave him a hard shove back, needing to work out some aggression and knowing Dante wouldn't mind.

He grabbed her wrists to pull her in for a kiss, but Colleen twisted at the last minute. Breaking his hold, she used his momentum to slam him face-first against the wall. She practiced judo every day with her bodyguard, Istvahn, an ex-Spetsnaz soldier who made sure Colleen could protect herself if he wasn't around.

"I don't have time to play with you." She pulled back on Dante's hair and spoke into his ear. He smelled nice; Dior's new men's fragrance, if she wasn't mistaken.

"Make time." He pushed away from the wall, quicker than she had been expecting.

They squared off. The slight fatigue disappeared in the surge of adrenaline. She wouldn't bottom for him, but if he'd let her throw him around, Colleen would consider getting sweaty with him. They circled each other. She was pretty sure he'd underestimate her, so they would have to work out a safe word and some parameters. It all seemed like too much work for too little effort, though.

"I'll have you begging for release," he vowed, and then spoiled the wonderful threat by tugging on his facial hair.

Visions of her being tied to a railroad track in a black-and-white film while a fast Charleston played made her smirk. Still, it was worth one last try to see how serious he wanted to play. Unlike the senator or the other Domme scenes she ran, if they were going to do this, she wanted complete control and at the end would satisfy herself with his body.

"I have a better idea," she said, stepping into his personal space again. "I'll strap you down and push every hard limit you have. Pegging, CBT, and anything else that crosses my evil little mind. If you survive, I'll ride you until you're hoarse from screaming."

Colleen watched his expression go from interest to horror and back to normal. He was at a loss for words. A small ping of disappointment pulsed through her. Eh, this was rapidly becoming boring. She was his boss. Either he'd hold back for fear of losing his job or he'd try to dominate her into giving him more power. It was one of the reasons she didn't screw around with the dungeon staff, no matter how tempting it was to teach an overconfident Dom what hard-core meant.

"You're the one who could use some punishment time," he said, folding his arms across his chest.

It was a lame comeback, more for his pride than for esca-lating whatever sexual tension she was trying to build.

Moving quickly, Colleen grasped his chin. Dante's jaw clenched, and his eyes went wide at the affront. "You're asking to be at the end of my whip."

"I dole out the discipline," he snarled, jerking out of her grip.

"Teach your class." She gave him a mild slap on the cheek and turned away from him.

"The next time, I'm not letting you off so easy." Colleen knew for a fact Dante didn't try this shit with any Club Inferno members, so she wasn't concerned for his professionalism. But lately he had seemed restless and been flirting with her more. As if he didn't have over twenty subs of his own to play with.

It wasn't that she wasn't tempted to give Dante a run for his money. It was the feeling that he'd be damned near insufferable if she ever submitted to him. He was already a little too full of himself.

Distracted, she walked into her office.

"Whoa!" Her administrative assistant, Nefertiti, held out a hand. "You've got a meeting with Couture people in fifteen minutes. A couple of models want to pitch a new workshop idea to you. I liked it. It's more of a business course about saving money and investing, but I think they could pull it off, so it's not snoresville. You, on the other hand, would make them clutch their pearls and shriek."

Colleen glanced down at her fetish wear. It was tame for her. Black thigh-high heeled boots, a spiked leather minidress, and matching gauntlets. "You don't think they'll buy that this is Gaultier's latest line?"

"I think they won't get past your tits playing peek-a-boo. Besides"—Nefertiti held her massively pregnant belly to make sure it cleared the desk as she got up from her chair —"you're seeing Chase Fairwood first."

Colleen felt hot and flushed, and then a chill trembled through her. "Oh, for God's sake, why?"

"He wants to discuss membership."

Shaking her head, she went through the inner door to her

office. "I'm sure you told him over my dead body. It's bad enough he shows up every time we have an open house."

Colleen strode into her office's bathroom and left the door ajar so she could talk to Nefertiti while she changed into a classy red vintage Valentino suit. Her ex-boyfriend—although boyfriend was too tame to describe their relationship—was trying to worm his way back into her life by throwing money around.

"I put him off the best I could," Nefertiti said from the other room. "But he says he has some tax questions about Mallory's shelter and clinic."

After wiggling into her beaded Manolos, Colleen stood up, smoothing her hand down the side of the suit. She nodded at her reflection before touching up her makeup.

"That's what he has lawyers and accountants for," Colleen said, coating her lipstick with a shimmer wand.

"His next excuse was he wanted to talk more in depth with Max about modeling for the activewear line. He thinks it would be easier if he had full access to Couture."

Colleen snorted as she finger-combed her hair. Chase had been a pro football player for several years until a vicious tackle bent his knee at an angle knees weren't meant to go in. He didn't need a modeling gig any more than she did. But Max, on the other hand, was married to her sister, Mallory. The same Mallory whose clinic Chase helped bankroll. Max was just starting out as a clothing designer, and Chase had decided to give Mallory's husband's clothing line a boost by adding the Chase Fairwood seal of approval. All because he wanted to get back into Colleen's life and most likely into her bed.

Not going to happen.

"He can't handle full access," Colleen said, wishing she could meet Chase in her bondage wear. She'd feel a little more in control. Or would she? A traitorous dampening in her panties made her think she'd cross a few lines with the man who had broken her heart. Colleen fiddled with the Club Inferno pin she'd placed on her lapel. She imagined Chase spread-eagled on the St. Andrew's cross, his chiseled ass red from a good spanking.

"Well, he keeps blowing up my phone, so I gave him the appointment to shut him up. It's up to you to shut him down."

Nefertiti's voice snapped Colleen out of the punishment fantasies, but not before they had heated up her imagination and distracted her with a slight ache between her legs. Damn Senator Clemmons. If he had just behaved, she'd at least have the calm centering that a successful scene gave her.

"Not a problem." Colleen said, both to her reflection and in answer to Nefertiti. Walking back into her office, Colleen got herself a diet cola out of the fridge and handed a vitamin-enhanced water to Nefertiti.

"No thanks." Nefertiti waved her off. "I'm going to barf."

Colleen checked the clock on the wall. "You're due for one."

"Morning sickness, my ass. Only the first trimester, my fat ass." Nefertiti hurried into Colleen's bathroom.

Colleen shut the door to give Nefertiti some privacy and to shut out the sound of her retching. As Colleen cracked open the soda, she fired up her computer to see if she could catch TMZ's latest report on her ex. She came up empty, but she did find one on herself.

"Don't these assholes ever get tired of the gold digger crap?" she muttered, and scanned the article. This time, it said, she had her sights on shipping mogul Bartholomew Kiryakius, whoever the hell that was. He made Alfie look like a spring chicken. At least the picture they posted of her was a good one. She had been coming out of Añejo, a tequila bar one of her Doms had opened. For once the camera didn't add ten pounds.

Because she still missed him every day, Colleen did a Google search for her husband, the late Alfred Granger, who had passed away four years ago at the age of eighty-one. A pang of sadness hit when his blue eyes twinkled back at her. Yes, he had been old enough to be her grandfather. Yes, he had been a billionaire. Yes, they'd met when she was working several jobs in Las Vegas. But she had loved him. He'd taught her everything she knew about being a Domme. He'd also saved her from loneliness, near poverty, and heartache.

The cause of that heartache was scheduled to walk into her office any minute now. Colleen got up and put an ear to her bathroom door. It sounded like Nefertiti was washing up. Walking over to the cabinet by the fridge, Colleen pulled out some crackers and spread peanut butter on them. She put them on a tray with grapes and small nibbles of cheese, placing the tray on Nefertiti's desk along with the flavored water, which she poured over ice.

"Thanks," Nefertiti said, coming out. She looked miserable, and she rubbed her stomach as if to soothe the savage beast inside.

Colleen frowned. "Why don't you—"

"Get back to work?" Nefertiti plopped down behind her desk. "What a good idea."

"I was going to say you should take a few hours off. Maybe get some rest?"

Nefertiti put her headset back on. "I'm good. Thanks for the grub." She popped a peanut butter cracker in her mouth and waved Colleen off.

Closing the door behind her, Colleen paced her office while she texted Istvahn, the father of Nefertiti's baby. In addition to being her bodyguard, he was also her chief of security.

She's eating. Still puking. Stubborn. Won't rest.

Colleen didn't expect him to answer, but she knew he liked to be kept in the loop. When he didn't buzz her back, she tossed the phone on her desk. If only Chase was content with text updates.

You're still a jerk. Die in a fire. Please.

The jealousy and pain still burned as fresh today as when she'd walked into his hotel room to find him covered with half-naked cheerleaders. Chase had been passed out drunk and didn't even wake up when she tossed the ice cubes from the bucket over all of them. The girls had taken one look at her and ran out of there as fast as their pom-poms would bounce.

Colleen had handled the rest of the breakup with aplomb, if not maturity. She'd taken her lipstick and written *Fuck you, asshole* on the mirror. Then she cut up all his credit cards and flushed them down the toilet. Chase had started to come around when she was stuffing his championship ring up his nose. So she gathered up all his clothes and threw them out the balcony window, and still managed to crack him one across the face before slamming out of the hotel room. That had been ten years ago. She'd married Alfie shortly after, and they'd had a good run. Alfie's health hadn't always allowed him to actively participate in sex, but he'd never given her a reason to feel neglected or worried that he would cheat on her.

When Nefertiti activated the intercom with a musical chime, Colleen hurried back to her chair so she could seem cool and composed when Chase came striding in. A former defensive tackle, he was tall and broad, muscled all over. Being out of the NFL for the past two years hadn't hurt his physique any. His sandy brown hair and boyish good looks had made him almost as popular as his sack record had. Chase eased himself into the chair across from her desk.

Why does he have to look so good?

"I'm glad you were able to find time to fit me into your busy schedule."

"Try to kiss me again and I'll have you thrown out," she warned him. The last time he had been here was before a concert. He had managed to corner her in the VIP booth. And because they couldn't be anywhere without fighting, their polite conversation had turned into a screaming match that ended up with them nearly fucking against the wall.

"No promises," he said, flashing his even white teeth.

She sighed. "What do you want?" The quicker she could get him out of here, the quicker she could get on with her life.

"You," he said simply. "You have to admit there's still chemistry."

Colleen angled her head in acknowledgment. They could set the drapes on fire. Right now, if she straddled his lap, they'd break the chair with their enthusiasm. It had always been like that. Hot, intense, deeply satisfying. She leaned back, crossing her own legs, and he tracked the smooth expanse of thigh she flaunted. "You have to admit there's still animosity," she pointed out. Just to tease him, she drew little circles on her thigh with her fingernails.

Chase wet his lips. "I'm willing to work on it, if you are."

She drained her soda and tossed the can in the trash. "I'm not." Been there, done that. And there weren't any Alfies waiting in the wings to rescue her this time.

"Okay," Chase agreed, crossing his own legs with a slight wince. "If you insist."

"How's the knee?" she asked, wishing the pang of sympathy would fuck off right alongside Chase Fairwood. He'd given in far too easily. He was up to something.

He shrugged. "Good days and bad days. I do like what

you're doing here. You always had an eye for fashion. I'm glad your husband indulged you to explore your talent."

Squinting at him, Colleen tried to find the sarcasm in the words he'd nearly said through his teeth. "You don't give a rat's ass about fashion. You wouldn't know a haute couture piece from a department store special."

"Want to put a little wager on that?"

Colleen wondered what his angle was. She inspected his jacket and suit pants. Chase had never been the type to wear edgy fashion; he had on a traditional Gucci suit and Fratelli Borgioli wing-tip dress shoes. He wore it well, too. Like he was on a job interview. If he had been applying for a security job, she might have hired him.

"I'm listening."

He tugged on the tie. Colleen wondered if he'd worn it just to impress her or if he really did want membership to Couture. She didn't see him as the type to lie around a fashion resort mingling with designers and models.

Well, maybe the models, she thought sourly.

"I don't want to be a sports announcer," Chase said, shifting so his bad knee was at a better angle. "Doing the convention circuit gets a little old. I don't have the chops to coach professionally. There's not much else. I was an athlete. It was all I ever wanted to be. I didn't bother to train in anything else. I got a free ride in college and was one of the first picked in the draft. I majored in communication, but that was so long ago everything is obsolete."

Colleen nodded at him to go on. None of this was news to her. "You could go back to college. Get another degree."

"In what?" Chase scoffed. He got up from the chair and headed over to the minibar set up in the corner. He had a slight limp she'd never noticed before. Colleen frowned and looked away, bothered that she cared.

"You could do security. You're big enough to be a bouncer. I wouldn't want to tangle with you."

"I'm a lover, not a fighter."

Colleen snorted.

"Besides," he continued, "I'm an easy target. All it would take is a hard shot to my knee, and 'Timber!' You got any beer?" Chase peered around the bar top.

"In the fridge."

"Sweet." He pulled out a bottle from one of the local microbreweries. He handed her another diet cola and she took it, making sure their fingers didn't touch.

"Get a degree in anything you want." Colleen tossed him a bottle opener from her desk drawer. "Law, business—hell, why not pre-med? You could go for a degree in sports medicine."

"I'm too old for that shit." He winged the bottle cap into the trash and took a long pull.

"Yeah, you're ancient."

"You like older men." Chase sat back down and threw her a smoky look that was just fringed with anger.

"Is that a shot at my husband?" Colleen's fingers itched for her riding crop.

"Why did you leave Vegas to go with him?"

Interesting. He'd never asked that question before. Had always danced around it. They were finally going to get into it. Colleen cracked her knuckles.

Let's finish this. Once and for all.

"I wanted to." Colleen shrugged. "He was good to me."

Chase's fingers tightened on the bottle and she thought for a minute there was going to be glass all over the floor, but he eased up. "It hadn't even been a month."

"A month since you cheated on me with half the cheer-leading squad." Coleen stabbed a finger in his direction.

"You cheated first." He leaned in over the desk, gently placing the bottle down.

"I did not," she shrieked in outrage, and slammed her fist on the desk.

Chase rescued the bottle before it toppled over and took another swig. "Whatever."

"No, not whatever," Colleen shouted. "You brought it up. Finish your bullshit line of logic." She was nearly blind with apoplexy. How dare he? How fucking dare he accuse her of that bullshit? She had been stupidly head-over-heels in love with him. Chase had been on the road with the team more often than he'd been in Vegas with her, and she'd never strayed. Not once. She hadn't ever been tempted. "Just because you have the morals of an alley cat, don't paint me with the same brush."

Easing back into his chair, he stared over her head out the floor-to-ceiling window. "Forget it."

"I never slept with anyone else while we were together."

"What about other things?" He put his left hand on his chest and did a Bill Clinton voice. "I did not have sexual relations with anyone."

"What the hell are you talking about, Chase?" Colleen resisted the urge to chuck the can of soda at his head.

"I saw you," he snarled, lunging across the desk so they were almost nose to nose.

"Saw me what?" She got right into his face and stared him down. Uh-oh. They were close enough to kiss. But what she wanted to do was nip at his lower lip, pull his hair, and go tumbling to the floor with him. This wasn't good.

"My buddies and I went to Miranda's Midnight House of Pain."

Colleen blinked. "Oh." She sank back into her chair, stunned. Not what she had been expecting him to say.

"Yeah." Chase gave a half laugh, returning to his own seat. "Oh." He swigged down some more beer.

"What does that have to do with anything?" She wasn't sure why he thought that had been cheating. The men hadn't been allowed to touch her. She had always been fully dressed —unlike the cocktail waitresses.

"Guess who the Mistress of Pain was the night we went?"

This didn't make sense. "You knew I had a bunch of odd jobs. I told you about being a phone sex operator. I told you I was training to be a professional dominatrix." Colleen racked her brain to see what pissed him off so bad about her working at Miranda's. Hell, the cocktail waitresses got more action than she had at that place. More tips, too.

"I thought the training wasn't so hands-on," he said.

"I didn't have sex with that man." Colleen swore in frustration. Now she was the one who sounded a little like Bill Clinton. "He never touched me. He paid to get flogged, and that's what I did."

"You were dressed like Catwoman, all in leather and showing so much skin you might as well have been naked."

"It was part of the fantasy. Jesus Christ, Chase, I was a stripper, too, and that didn't bother you. What's the deal?"

"The deal was I never went to the club you were stripping at with my friends."

Colleen's lips tightened, and she felt the alarming prick of tears at the corner of her eyes. "You were ashamed of me." She blinked rapidly to get rid of the traitorous liquid. Only Chase could bring her from lust to anger to tears in less than ten minutes. To be fair, he could also bring joy and laughter, but it had been a long, long time since they were anything but adversaries.

"No." Chase shook his head. "Embarrassed. I didn't want the guys to recognize you, but of course they did. You weren't wearing a mask."

"I wasn't hiding," she said through her teeth. "And I wasn't cheating on you."

"It looked more intimate than stripping." He folded his arms across his chest and let out a big sigh.

"It is," Colleen said, and thought of the senator again. The bond between Domme and sub didn't have to be sexual. In most cases it was, but more often than not it was mostly about letting go of control and trusting that it'd be safe to indulge in dark fantasies that the mainstream population wouldn't understand. Safe, sane, and consensual was the code she lived by. "A pro Domme usually doesn't have sex with her clients."

"Usually?" Chase snarled.

"I didn't have sex with my clients. I didn't jerk them off. I didn't suck them off. I didn't fuck them raw. Is that clear enough for you?"

"Whatever," Chase said.

"Don't be a passive-aggressive asshole. You started this." Colleen crossed her arms over her chest. "Explain how you think our breakup was all my fault."

"I got pissed. Paid you back with the cheerleaders. I figured we'd get over our mad and go on from there."

"Except I didn't do anything wrong." Colleen had to try hard not to crumple her can in frustration.

He gave another half laugh. "Turns out I didn't, either. I was too drunk to get it up."

It felt like time had stopped. Colleen wasn't sure she was even breathing anymore. For the past ten years she had been able to cope with losing Chase because she thought he had been untrue. Her heart beat loud in her chest. For a moment she got lost in his hazel eyes. They were flecked with gold and green. It was getting hard to breathe because it felt like a boa constrictor was squeezing her chest.

"I'm not saying that when I sobered up and the chicks

were still there that I wouldn't have tried to get even. But then you were there. Did you have to leave me naked and broke?"

"Yes," Colleen said. The pain in her chest was fading away to numbness. Two prideful idiots—that's what they had been. Communication never had been their strong point.

"You nearly broke my jaw." Chase rubbed it as if it still hurt.

"Good." *You broke my heart.* She almost rubbed her chest at the phantom pain. Then she shook herself out of the stupor and went for the attack again. She couldn't let her guard down around him. "And I think you're glossing over the fact that you and I were in a committed relationship and you felt it was all right to go out to a BDSM show with your friends."

He snorted. "You didn't care about shit like that."

"Then don't play the double-standard card."

"I was there for the beer and to hang out with my friends," he said.

Now it was her turn to snort. "Then you could have picked a thousand other casino bars. You picked a sex show and you had the nerve to be pissed at me?"

"I wasn't up there with my tits on display crawling around a bare-assed tourist."

"You could have been." Colleen shrugged. "Hell, you could have been the tourist. We asked for volunteers from the audience. Why didn't you just wait for me backstage instead of pulling a hissy and staying out all night? I could have shown you the difference between sex and dominance."

Still could. But they were having this conversation ten years too late.

"Because by the time I got over being angry, you had moved to Texas with that old fart."

Colleen held up a hand. "Don't you ever say anything against Alfie."

17

Chase pushed to his feet. "Yeah, he was a real saint."

"I'm warning you, Chase."

He finished his drink staring at the wall. Tossed the bottle into the trash, where the bottle shattered.

"Everything all right in there?" Istvahn's voice grumbled over the intercom.

"Fine," she said, toggling the speaker off. Nefertiti must have called him in when their voices got too loud.

Closing her eyes, Colleen tried to drive back the if-onlys. "Let's try and get this conversation back on track." She needed to get him the hell out of her office until this vulnerable and achy feeling went away. "Why do you want to be a full member of Couture? You're not a designer."

"I like the idea of being a clothes hanger." He hung his arms out like he was the Scarecrow in *The Wizard of Oz*.

She smirked. "You're too big for most designers."

"Most. Not for your brother-in-law's line."

"As much as I like Max's designs, he's just starting out."

"So am I." Chase spread his arms in a large shrug.

"You can't be his clothes hanger exclusively." Colleen tapped a pen on her ledger. "If you're serious about a career in modeling, I can make a few calls and get you some interviews with agencies."

"I've got an agency. They're searching for opportunities for me, but they said it couldn't hurt to get some experience. So I figure having a membership here would look great on my resume. If it's the money, I can pay triple the fee, or pay for membership in full a year in advance."

"It's not about the money, Chase."

"Of course not. Granger hooked you up when he croaked."

Slamming the pen down, she got up from her desk. "Get the fuck out of my office. I don't need to hear shit like that from the likes of you."

He held up his hands in surrender. "You're right. I'm being a dick. I just can't picture you and him together."

"So stop picturing it. Stop thinking about me in bed with anyone. It's ancient history."

"It doesn't have to be."

"Yeah, it pretty much does," Colleen said. Especially if he got freaked out over Miranda's Midnight House of Pain. "You're going to have to trust me that joining Couture would be a big mistake."

"Why?"

Colleen considered how much she wanted to tell him. "Couture is a lot of things to a lot of people," she hedged. "There are areas that you would be prohibited from entering, and I know you, Chase—you'd keep at it until you uncovered every last secret corner. Quite frankly, you'd be disappointed with what you find."

Some of the dungeon scenes made Miranda's Midnight House of Pain look like *Little House on the Prairie*. Actually, some of them were based on *Little House on the Prairie*. Pa and Nellie cosplay was more popular than one would think.

"I'm a sophisticated world traveler." He came around the desk.

"You're an ape in a twenty-five-hundred-dollar suit." She met him chest to chest. Unlike when she was close to Dante, Colleen's heart was racing, and she craved the danger that was coming off him in waves.

"What are you afraid of?" He dragged her against him so hard her feet nearly came out of her Manolos.

Losing my heart again.

Colleen could have stepped on his expensive leather shoes with her sharp heel. She could have lifted her knee and nailed him one in the jewels. Hell, Istvahn was just a shout away. But Colleen lifted her arms around his neck and met his mouth with a savage lust that propelled them back into the wall.

Just this one kiss.

The morning's frustration with the senator and Dante vanished under the heavy press of Chase's mouth. He tangled his fingers up in her hair, holding her head at an angle that was just short of pain. She pressed her belly into his erection. The hard, hot length of him made her want to toss him to the floor and have her way with him.

Why not?

A traitorous thought. She moaned into his mouth. Colleen hadn't indulged herself since letting go her last sex slave. Lust and deprivation caused this. She ruled the nightlife of the hottest sex club in the country, but the last time she'd gotten laid was sometime last season. There was always a crisis to handle, always a problem to fix. No men measured up to her standards, and training a new slave was becoming too much like work. But here in Chase's arms, with his tongue filling her mouth, all that existed was the two of them.

He reached under her suit's skirt, pushed aside the thong.

Colleen hooked her leg around his knee to give him better access, even as she muttered, "Damn you."

When he dipped a finger inside her molten heat, she tightened her leg.

His flinch was a dash of cold water, and she shoved away from him.

"That's my bad knee," he said, bringing his finger up to his mouth to taste her. "You taste like honey."

She watched his talented tongue swirl around, licking her wetness off his finger, and she nearly went back for more.

Don't be an idiot.

"You're going to have two bad knees if you don't stop kissing me," she warned, heading toward the door. She was still shaking with the need to strip them both and spend the afternoon having wild sex.

Why not? rang in her head again.

"Stop fighting yourself, Colleen. We're older. Wiser. You're a rich widow and I'm a washed-up ball player. Why not give us a second chance?"

Colleen's hand was on the doorknob as she considered his words. "Chase, I'm not who you think I am." Hell, if she thought he could handle it, she'd drag him down to the dungeon right now and show him what he was missing. But it would only solidify in his mind that she had been cheating on him all those years ago. She couldn't go back to vanilla sex and be satisfied. He would need to accept the kink that ruled her sex life. And accept her dominating him.

Would he?

Colleen's eyes narrowed. It might work—if she came on strong enough that he just reacted to her instead of thinking about what she was doing.

There was that one night when they were drunk and she'd sat on his face and nearly smothered him while she came. While he had been gasping for breath, she switched positions on him. Rode his cock, just using him to come again. Colleen licked her lips.

"What are you thinking about?" His voice was low and dirty. Chase crossed the room to her.

She tossed her suit jacket on the chair. It was too warm in here. Her breasts ached and her pussy throbbed from the memory of that hot night. What had come after involved candle wax and rough sex.

Yeah, he liked the kink that night.

Of course, he had tied her up with his belt, not the other way around.

"Let's get to know each other all over again. This"—Chase gestured between them—"is something I have never felt with anyone else." He cupped her face in his hands. Kissed her sweetly. A soft brush of his lips that burned into her heart. "I want you."

Damn it. The feeling is mutual.

"You think you want me," she said. "But you can't handle me."

She wanted to make him pay for those cheerleader skanks. Colleen wanted to tie him down to the bed and force him to make it up to her before she allowed him to come.

"Try me." He muscled her flat against the door with a heavy thump. She fought the urge to giggle hysterically because she was pretty sure Nefertiti had an ear to the door.

"You're going to be disappointed. And I won't let you hurt me again." Colleen crossed her arms over her chest.

Chase uncrossed them and held her arms captive over her head.

Oh no. You didn't.

But this time his kiss was all persuasion instead of demand. Colleen let him hold her still because she wanted the magic his mouth promised. But if he thought this was the norm, she was going to have him on his knees. If she wouldn't bottom for an experienced Dom, she'd be damned if she'd let Chase Fairwood call all the shots in the bedroom.

And that's when it hit her. She was actually considering this. Maybe she could have Chase, play with him, and dominate him. In the end, he'd leave because it wasn't his kink to be submissive. And in the meantime, she could get this lust, this leftover emotion from her long-dead past, out of both their systems.

"That's an evil grin," he said, kissing the corner of her mouth.

"You want a shot at me?" she asked, pulling her arms out of his grip.

"More than anything." He rubbed her bottom lip with his thumb. She bit it. "Ow, you like to bite?"

You have no idea.

"Come to the Hot Spot Friday night," she said, referring to Couture's sexy dance club. On normal nights, it was just beautiful people drinking Cristal and being seen. But once a month she turned up the heat to see if any of her fashionistas were interested in a wilder version of play. If they were, they might be interviewed to have access to Club Inferno, the dungeons below the fashion resort.

"I'll make sure the bouncers know to admit you. We're having a special party. It's guaranteed to blow your mind. If you can handle it, we'll talk about taking it to the next level. But I think you're in way over your head, Fairwood."

"If I spend all night with you at the dance club, you'll give me a membership to Couture?" He angled his head at her. "My knee won't let me dance for very long."

"Then you can sit and watch." Colleen opened the door. "Take it or leave it."

"Oh, I'll take it," he vowed. Trailing his fingers over her cheek, he blew her a kiss and walked out.

CHAPTER 2

"Go back to the part where he Dommed you," Anya said. "Because that's never going to get old."

It was midweek, and Colleen sat across from her best friend, picking at her cucumber yogurt salad. They were at Couture's Middle Eastern restaurant having lunch before the launch of their Fierocity clothing line. Anya was digging into her chicken shawarma as if the fate of the project they'd spent most of the year on wasn't about to be attacked by viperous harpies who made Internet trolling an art form.

"He still thinks I'm this stupid twenty-year-old piece of fluff who gets all wiggly-kneed when he flexes his muscles."

Anya shrugged. "At least he doesn't think you're a thirty-year-old dipshit."

"How can you sit there and be so calm?" Colleen pointed an accusatory fork at her.

"Because I go for my final fitting with Marisol after lunch. So even if I'm a little bloated, she'll sew around the poofiness." Anya poked at her tummy. "Also Spanx, baby."

Colleen held her head. "I need a paper bag."

"To barf or blow in?"

"To put over my head if this thing tanks."

Anya tapped her fork on her plate. "So what if it does? Chalk it up as a loss and move on to the next big thing in your life. What is it this week? Licorice bindings for the sub with a sweet tooth? Lighten up. You're the idea chick."

Colleen didn't want to tell her that lately the ideas had been drying up and the past few failures had really shaken her confidence. It seemed like she was the media's favorite object to ridicule, like a living dumb-blond joke.

"What if you get out there in our pink skull suit and they boo? Or worse, laugh? Or worse than that, don't pay attention?"

Anya ticked off the responses on her fingers. "If they boo, I'll shoot them the bird or flash them a tit. If they laugh, I'll have Clint beat them up. And if they don't pay attention, I'll do a strip tease."

Colleen raised her head, horrified, until she saw the laughter in Anya's expression.

"Chill out, Colleen. I've got this. I've modeled uglier shows for nastier audiences."

"What if that bitch who blogged that Bar Refaeli looked like a heifer stampeding on the runway is here?"

Anya blew a raspberry. "Like that jealous turd could even get into Couture. I know you're press shy because of TMZ being all up in your Kool-Aid at every turn, but don't make yourself crazy about the press."

"I can just see the headlines: 'Gold-Digging Whore Fails Again.'" Colleen framed the words in the air.

"Oh, come on, you're not a gold digger." Anya smiled. "Whore, on the other hand, is accurate."

Colleen stuck her tongue out at her. "Don't try and make me feel better. I'm having an anxiety attack over here."

"No, you're not. And if you'd ever had one, you wouldn't compare it to this little self-pity party. Suck it up, buttercup.

They'll like it or they'll hate it. If they hate it, we'll think of something else. With your bank, we can keep trying until we get it right."

Colleen nodded, conceding the point. "I just want the recognition that I'm not only Alfie Granger's bimbo wife."

"You've got it," Anya said. "The people who matter already know that. You have a thriving business as a resort owner. Your members-only sex club is blooming. I can't believe you managed to keep Club Inferno on the down-low the way you have. I figured Rita would have at least spilled the beans."

"Rita knows I'd crush her like a bug. Our nondisclosure agreement is fuck-me-at-your-own-peril."

"I love it when you talk dirty." Anya grinned.

Anya still hadn't forgiven her old rival Rita for trying to bust up her relationship with Clint, one of Club Inferno's Doms.

"We've got a good membership," Colleen said. "They like having the exclusive pleasure rooms. They like being part of an elite group. It's me that can't seem to settle down to one thing."

"You want it all." Anya shrugged. "Nothing wrong with that."

"I don't know what I want," Colleen said.

"You put a lot of pressure on yourself to be the head honcho. The ice queen bitch who stands alone and wields a baton of smacking."

"A what?" Colleen wrinkled her forehead.

Anya held out a hand. "I'm rolling. Keep up. What you need is a vacation."

"I can't leave now. Nefertiti's about to pop. Istvahn is worried sick. I'm short two Doms because of you and Mallory marrying them, and now all they want to do is play kissy face with you instead of spank and punish for my club. Dante is just begging for a chance to get into my stilettos."

"Kinky."

"You know what I mean. If I give him an inch, he'll be in my office with his feet on my desk telling me to run along like a good little girl while he manages my dungeons."

"You're a control freak," Anya stage-whispered.

"No shit," Colleen whispered back.

"Okay, so if you can't get away to some tropical paradise, why don't you relax here? Enjoy the Club you put together instead of micromanaging the Doms."

"Did Clint say that?" Colleen put a hand to her heart, a sharp stab of hurt hitting her harder because she hadn't been expecting the criticism.

"No, of course not. Everybody loves you and is a little afraid of you."

"Oh," Colleen said, mollified. "Good." Fear and admiration were what made her black heart tingle, after all.

"Listen," Anya said, "why don't you go down to the dungeon now? Take some you-time, and maybe show Master Dante a thing or two?" She waggled her eyebrows. "And let me know all the details."

"You want details on Dante, fuck him yourself." Colleen grinned.

"Yeah, like that would fly with Clint. Besides, I don't want to fuck Master Dante. I just want to know how he is in bed."

"I'm sure he'll let you watch."

"That's what I'm afraid of. He still scares the shit out of me."

"Wimp," Colleen scoffed.

"You know it." Anya wiped her mouth with the napkin and pushed back from the table. "I gotta go catch up with Marisol before she sends Istvahn to find me. Remember, relax. Breathe. We've got this."

Colleen nodded, but her heart wasn't in it. She forced herself to stay for a cup of coffee while she doodled on her sketch pad. It didn't help with her nerves. So she signed off on the check and went down to Club Inferno.

At this time of the day, there were mostly sex workshops going on. All of her Doms did double duty as instructors and taught classes in their specialty. Clint taught stripping. Max demonstrated his Japanese rope bondage skills. Micah educated interested members on the joys and dangers of electrical stimulation and knife play. Dante did erotic asphyxiation and orgasm denial.

These are a few of my favorite things, she hummed to herself as the elevator took her into the underground levels of the club.

Maybe some whip practice would ease her nerves. She keyed open her private dungeon and changed out of her prim and proper suit. Some nights when she was lonely, she slept down here and masturbated to the sounds of pleasure. Flipping through her closet, Colleen slipped into a leather catsuit.

The dungeon was set up for her next client appointment. Whereas the Doms taught group classes, Colleen did private sessions. Tomorrow she was meeting with a married couple who were learning anal play together. This was their third session, and Colleen was anticipating taking them to the next level. In the first class she'd had the husband go down on his wife while he played with his wife's anus. Then they'd switched. The husband had been a little wary about it, but the blow job really relaxed him into enjoying his wife rimming him with a well-lubed finger. The next session, Colleen had made them wear butt plugs while they made love. Their homework for the week had been to use the plugs every night. Colleen had something special waiting for them tomorrow. On their application, they had said they liked to role-play and pretend forced consent. She was going to take that to a level that she was hoping would both shock and turn them on.

The dungeon was set up like a prison, complete with orange jumpsuits and cheap cots. They were going to take turns having prison sex with each other, engaging in anal penetration—him with his cock and her with a strap-on dildo. It should be a lot of fun. Colleen was going to lock them in together until they came twice each.

After a last-minute check to see if she had enough lube and baby wipes and that everything was cleansed to her satisfaction, Colleen secured the dungeon and headed to another one of her private areas, her whip room. She wound up passing by Dante's class. One of his favorite subs, Jana, was on her knees, her head down and knees spread. Dante was talking about orgasm control. His other favorite sub, Leo, was chained to the wall while another of Club Inferno's subs was giving him a fast and furious blow job.

"Please, Master, may I come?" Leo begged.

Colleen felt a small smile perk up her face. Leo was a good sub. She resisted the urge to play with him herself. This was Dante's class, and she wasn't that much of an egomaniac to walk in and interrupt.

"No," Dante said, walking up and down the ranks of students who were stroking and rubbing each other.

"Master, please. I'm going to come." Leo breathed fast and hard. A fine sheen of sweat coated his chest and abs.

"Stop." The sub at Leo's feet immediately removed her mouth from his cock.

Leo hissed a breath and held himself back.

Colleen leaned against the door frame to enjoy the show. If it was up to her, she'd put Leo on his knees and have him persuade her to let him get off. But she didn't have a sex slave. At least not yet. She tried to picture Chase in Leo's position. She'd have to secure Chase. He didn't have Leo's control. The thought made her breath quicken.

"Good." Dante clapped his hands, and Colleen jumped a little guiltily. But he wasn't talking to her.

One of his students had raised his hand, and Dante nodded at him.

"I thought the whole purpose of this was to come. I mean, if that hot little redhead was on my dick, I'd be off in a shot."

"Speed isn't a skill."

The class laughed, and the questioner turned a deep shade of red.

Leo gave out a soft whimper.

Dante backhanded him across the face.

The class gasped, but Colleen knew a pulled shot when she saw it. The blow was all noise and a sting. Leo wanted another, by the way his hips shifted. Dante, knowing his sub, backhanded him again. This time Leo's head swung the other way. They were playing to the crowd and enjoying themselves in the process.

Colleen glanced down at Jana to see if she was getting turned on. Leo and Jana were lovers. But there was something off about Jana.

"Thank you, Sir," Leo cried.

But Colleen wasn't watching him anymore. Jana was shifting, which was almost unheard of. She was one of the best-trained subs Colleen had ever met. Not to mention she was so utterly devoted to Dante she'd do anything for him. Colleen walked into the room to get a better look.

Dante glanced over his shoulder, did a double take at her, and smiled. "Ladies and gentlemen, our hostess graces us with her presence. Mistress, welcome." He gave her a deferential nod.

"Continue," Colleen said, standing next to Jana.

"When you deny yourself something, it becomes sweeter,"

Dante said, turning back to his class. "Who here has given up something for Lent or maybe a New Year's resolution?"

There were a few nods.

"Imagine denying yourself chocolate for a year. How does that first bite taste?"

"Orgasmic," a woman sighed.

"Master, are you saying we have to abstain for a whole year?" A man in the background sounded horrified.

As Dante answered him that it all depended on the results they wanted, Colleen peered down at Jana. Sweat was dripping down her face.

"Dante, I'm taking control of your sub." Colleen reached down and plucked an unresisting Jana up to a standing position. She sagged in relief against Colleen.

He broke off at her rude interruption and whirled on her. Then he took in Jana's posture and stepped in toward them. "Are you all right?" He lifted up Jana's chin with two fingers.

"Please, Master, may I go with Mistress Colleen?"

"Yes," Dante said, and threw a worried glance at Colleen.

"Continue," she told him again, more curtly than she wanted to. It was one thing to interrupt another Dom's scene on a whim, but this was a safety issue. Ushering Jana out of the room, Colleen checked to see if Jana had any bindings on her. "Are you wearing a corset? Do you have any ropes on you?"

"No, ma'am. I'm not feeling well." Jana rubbed her stomach.

"Why didn't you let Dante know?"

"I didn't want to interrupt him."

"You'd rather pass out in front of the class?" Colleen asked, fighting the urge to shake the woman.

"Please, Ma'am. I need to go to the bathroom," Jana blurted out.

"Go." Colleen shoved her toward the nearest one, and Jana ran.

Colleen waited outside. If Jana was pregnant, Colleen was going to stop drinking the water around here. After fifteen minutes, Jana slunk out.

"Please don't be mad at him, Mistress," she begged, and started to slink down to her knees, but Colleen caught her, hauling Jana back up to her feet.

"What's going on?" Colleen demanded.

"I had some sketchy sushi last night."

Colleen closed her eyes. "Are you sure it's not something else?"

"What?"

Colleen opened her eyes and mimed an expanding belly.

"Oh, hell no. Ma'am. No, ma'am. I'm unable." Jana looked away quickly and swallowed hard.

"I see," Colleen said, feeling like an ass for jumping to conclusions. "Very well. Go up to your room and rest for eight hours. Once the sushi has left your system you can report back to your Master."

"No, she can't," Dante said, approaching them at a fast clip.

"Master, I'm so sorry." Jana fell at his feet and began to kiss his boots.

"Stop," he said.

She obeyed instantly.

"You were given instruction. Don't shame me even further than you have."

"I'm so sorry, Master." Jana scurried to her feet.

"After you rest, you are to attend to Mistress Colleen's every need for twenty-four hours."

Colleen opened her mouth to protest but shut it at Dante's furious glare. It was his sub, and besides, Nefertiti could use the help. Jana's idea of serving was usually sexual, so being forced into business attire and helping around the office was a pretty good punishment.

"Yes sir," Jana said miserably, and retreated out of the dungeon.

"I should have caught that." Dante rubbed his temples.

Colleen shrugged. "It happens. I'm glad it wasn't anything more serious than bad sushi. But . . ." Colleen put her hand on his shoulder. "She needs to feel it's all right to interrupt you in an emergency."

"I'll work on it," he said. "And I'll pay more attention to her. Jana's just so well trained I've gotten lazy."

"Don't be so hard on yourself. It's not as if you were chucking knives at her this time."

Dante chuckled and followed her as she continued to her whip room. Inside, several whips in various lengths and styles were hung up on pegs or lovingly placed in velvet bags. She couldn't wait to hear the satisfying crack as she practiced her figure eights and volleys.

Colleen fondled a few leather whips, considering each one for length before choosing a ten-foot bullwhip specially made and modified by one of the greatest whip makers in the world, David Morgan. She heard the Indiana Jones theme song in her head every time she picked this one up. It had been Alfie's.

"Where's Leo?" she asked.

"I've let the students play with him and each other for a while." At her raised eyebrow, he clarified. "Micah is supervising. I wanted to catch up with you."

"Well, as you can see, I'm going to need a lot of room, so carry on with whatever you have to do." Poking around for some cards to put on the targeting form, Colleen came across some candles. She could light them and see if she could snuff them out with the tip of the whip. But she would have to let them burn a little. Some hot wax on her nipples might be a way to end this solo scene.

"I'd like to watch you work."

Colleen considered it. It might be fun to have an audience. "Okay. But I'm warning you, Dante," she said, waving him back, "the range on this thing is longer than you think. Don't move once I start winding up."

Without answering, he went to a closet and shrugged into a heavy leather jacket.

Colleen swallowed hard. "What are you doing?"

He pulled a St. Andrew's cross to the center of the room. "I thought about what you said before. Maybe you should teach me a lesson. I want to see how you work. Buckle me on."

Colleen swore. "Talk about topping from the bottom."

Dante had the grace to smile sheepishly. "Twenty whacks with that whip," he said, doing it again.

Colleen inspected the tip. Shaking her head, she said, "This whip will cut that jacket to shreds. It's too heavy for people play." She pouted a bit, but put it back in favor of another single-tail whip. This one was shorter, about six feet in length, and also made out of kangaroo leather.

"I can take it."

"Maybe we can work up to it." Dante had no idea what he was asking for. Colleen considered it, though. With a heavier and lined jacket, it would still hurt like a bitch, but it wouldn't draw blood.

She unrolled the smaller bullwhip and tested the weight, gave it a few cracks. "Even with that jacket on, this is still going to leave marks."

"Good. Now, make it hurt. If you can."

Oh, this was even better than him watching her pretend to be Lady Zorro. Colleen didn't hesitate to take him up on it. She knew Dante had a high tolerance for pain and was more than capable of taking a whipping. If he wanted some of this, she'd gladly give it to him. Strapping his arms and legs down, she slapped his ass. "Safe word?"

"Don't need one."

"You're getting one anyway. 'Jana' is what you say when you've had enough." Colleen checked the jacket's thickness. Dante was going to have a back full of bruises. But he knew that. So she wasn't going to hold his hand through it. Still, she needed to let him know the score.

"I'm not going to go easy on you," she warned. "I can always smack the hell out of my practice dummy if you change your mind. Are you sure you want this?"

"Yes, Ma'am." He rested his cheek against the frame.

"Oh, I was wondering if you knew that word." Her sarcasm was lost on him.

He closed his eyes and relaxed into the cross like he was taking a nap. Thick black lashes rested on his cheeks. He really was quite pretty.

Colleen went back to warming up, a thrill of anticipation flooding through her. She loved her bullwhips, but she rarely got to take them out to play. Most beginning submissives who liked flogging preferred cats and quirts the best. The more experienced ones would let her use a signal whip. The bullwhip was as powerful as it sounded, but truthfully the fun sonic boom sound was what really pushed people's buttons, and all whips did that. Colleen wound up and did some practice cracks until Dante stopped flinching from the snap. She rolled her shoulder, feeling it loosen up. It was going to be marvelous not to hold back.

"Ready?"

"Whip me, beat me, make me write bad checks," he joked.

She let loose in the center of his back.

His laugh turned into a shout of surprise and pain.

"You okay?" she asked.

Dante breathed out through his teeth. "A softer blow might have been nicer to start with."

"You're wearing armor, you big pussy." She wound up and took him again in the back an inch below the first strike.

"Fuck," he snarled.

"Oh, that reminds me," Colleen said, cracking the whip over his head, enjoying his flinch. "I'm not fucking you after this."

He grunted, tensing for the next blow, which she made him wait for. She flicked it past his arm, missing him by calculated inches.

"You know what you're doing, right?" he asked as she cracked the whip by his ear.

"The time to ask that, Dante, was before you demanded to be strapped in." She landed another hard stroke on his back, an inch lower than the last.

Gritting his teeth, he hissed out between breaths, "I figured you knew enough to hit my back."

"You're a dumb-ass. This whip in the hands of an amateur is dangerous; deep cuts would be the least of your worries." And for shits and giggles, she put another strike close to the back of his thigh. While she was pretty sure she could snap it just below his balls, she never played that dangerous. Never wanted to risk an injury there. "How are you doing?"

"Is that all you got?"

"The correct phrase is 'Thank you, Mistress.'"

"You hit like a girl."

He wasn't flip anymore after three precise lashes landed on his shoulders in quick succession. She let him recover, his slight moans not affecting her libido in the slightest. But there was a sense of pride, and something tight in her chest loosened. Anya had been right: she needed to let go. Colleen was rolling up the bullwhip when Dante roused out of the haze of pain she put him in.

"We're not finished, are we?" he said groggily.

She must be cursed to have lousy subs. Uncuffing him long enough to slide the jacket off him, Colleen checked his back. Deep welts were beginning to form.

"Looks good," she told him, using her hand to give him another hard whack on his ass.

He didn't even respond to the tap. "Why are we stopping?" he asked in a gruff voice.

She really needed to get a nice quiet submissive. "Think you can take twenty lashes with a bullwhip, tough guy?"

"I took six."

"Six is all you're going to take. I need you mobile and functioning tomorrow. As it is, you're going to be sore." She secured him back to the cross.

He shifted restlessly. "So untie me then," he said sourly.

"I didn't say we were done," Colleen said, grabbing a flogger with suede falls to lessen the impact.

CHAPTER 3

C hase could count on one hand the number of fucks he gave about fashion designers and models who looked like they could use a double cheeseburger and gravy fries. He was on his best behavior, trying to appear interested, nodding in all the right places when one or the other came up to him and prattled on about things that were as foreign to him as one of Gregg Williams's blitz schemes would be to them.

What he did care about had just sauntered in like the pussycat who'd licked the cream. Colleen eased into her seat and crossed those gorgeous legs. As discreetly as he could, Chase adjusted himself. What he wouldn't give to shimmy her out of that prissy skirt and taste her again, this time with those legs wrapped over his shoulders instead of his bad knee.

The hard aluminum chair was made for short events. This fashion show was already going on too long, and it hadn't even started yet. Chase paid little attention to the introductory speeches until Colleen got up on the stage. The hope that she would be modeling some of the designs—especially lingerie—died when she just gave good promo and thanked her staff.

His staff, on the other hand, enjoyed seeing the slight peek of cleavage as she sat back down again. He had it bad, but if it had been all one-sided, he would have walked away without a second glance. Colleen wanted him, too. Her kisses proved it. They just had so much bad blood between them, he wasn't sure they'd ever get past it.

As it was, he still got razzed by his buds about being a whipping boy. He wondered if those assholes jacked off to the memory of Colleen in that tight leather costume, which had made her ass look like a heart-shaped pillow he wanted to fuck. God knew he still did. And when she had turned around, her breasts almost spilling out of that damned corset, he knew before he saw her face it had been his girlfriend his buddies were lusting over. It took them a few minutes to realize it. Probably because those jerks were fixated on the most perfect set of tits on the planet. After that, it had been all dildos in his locker and whips coiled up in his helmet.

He wasn't into all that freaky stuff. It didn't make sense to him. He'd lived with too much pain after his injury to even contemplate that it could get his dick hard. What was wrong with just plain fucking?

Chase forced himself to look at the clothes that the models were parading up and down the runway in. It looked good to him, not that he knew anything about fashion. He could picture Colleen lounging around in some of the outfits. Glancing around, Chase noticed a few people typing or texting furiously into their devices. Flashbulbs went off so frequently, it was like being in a rave. It seemed as though Fierocity was a success.

He was glad for her. As much as he admired her kicking body, he knew she could be more than arm candy for an eighty-year-old letch. Colleen was as smart as she was beautiful, running the chain of hotels that Granger's family had let her have after she agreed to leave the family quietly and quickly. It must have stung for her to pack up and leave her home.

Or maybe she'd been glad to go.

The thought that she'd married the old man because she was running away from Chase made him feel like a grade-A loser. He needed to know what the story was between Colleen and her Texas billionaire. Maybe Granger had married her just to show off and to piss off his kids. Lord knew she was easy on the eyes.

His teammates had gotten nasty about her after he had to call one of them to help him find his clothes after Colleen destroyed his hotel room. Then when she'd married Granger, all bets were off. Every tabloid picture or stupid report had been pasted in his locker. He hadn't been able get away from her even if he tried. It'd died down after a year or so, but when the old man died of a heart attack, it started up all over again. The gossip was he died after having sex with his young wife. Colleen had become the brunt of a lot of locker room jokes again. A part of him had wanted to stick up for her, but self-preservation had quelled that little spark. He wasn't proud of it, but eventually the team had moved on to other targets.

She'd never really left his thoughts, not even when his teammates forgot about it and went on to easier targets. Sure, there'd been other women—a lot of other women—but none of them interested him enough to offer more than a tumble or two. Then when he'd had his career-ending accident, the women stopped coming around. He'd like to think

Colleen wouldn't have left him at his lowest point. She wasn't a quitter. She was a fighter.

He grinned, thinking about how pissed she had been that day in the hotel room when she caught him in bed with the cheerleaders. If she had only stayed to listen, or maybe if he had let her explain . . . Chase's smile died. Well, maybe she would have been his wife instead of Granger's. He wasn't a multibillionaire, but they would have had a nice life, even after his accident.

Absently massaging his knee, he remembered the lonely days in the hospital and the agony of the physical therapy. Had any of the party girls stopped by? Not that he could remember. His only visitors had been his sister and nephew, and while that was nice, he missed his friends. But they had been on the road, trying to get into the playoffs without him.

Max slid into the chair next to Chase. He taught martial arts classes to the fashion models when he wasn't working on his own designs. Chase thought he was a pretty solid guy and admired that he ignored all the blatant come-ons from women—because he was happily married to Colleen's sister.

"Can you see yourself up there?" Max asked.

Chase glanced up and was surprised to see Colleen's old roommate from her Vegas days strutting down the runaway. He racked his brain to come up with her name. Amy? Anna? Anya? That was it. "I don't have the legs for that dress," he said.

Anya whirled and gave them a peek at the red bows at the top of her garters. Wow. He'd like to see a pair of those on Colleen, preferably as she was bent over her desk.

"Think you can walk the walk?"

Chase laughed. "I'll give it a shot, but don't make me wear silk stockings."

"Good," Max said. "After this is over, there are a few

buyers I want you to meet. They're going to be pushing hard for your endorsement. Cardboard cutouts in their stores, autograph sessions, and the like."

"Not a problem," he assured the other man. That was all part of his plan. Get in the stores and magazines. Maybe promote his own brand of merchandise. He had offers, but he wanted his name on something more meaningful than mud flaps and beer cozies. A watch sponsorship would be nice, like the one Eli Manning had. Then again, he hadn't been a quarterback. He should probably hedge his bets. "But you might want to get a pretty girl to sell the line with me. What about your wife?"

Max snorted. "I won't tell her you said that."

"Good." He rubbed his nose. "It still hurts from the last time she sucker-punched me."

He was glad the little firecracker found someone to look out for her. Mallory had been a teenager when he first met her, and he'd always had a soft spot for her, like she was his baby sister, too.

Could have been, if I hadn't fucked things up.

Max was talking about scheduling, but Chase was only listening with half an ear. A man he didn't recognize had come up to Colleen. He moved stiffly, as if he was in pain. But what had caught his attention was that he leaned down and kissed Colleen's cheek. She smiled up at him and patted the seat next to her. Her hand was resting on the son of a bitch's knee.

"Who's that?" Chase interrupted Max.

"Huh?"

Chase gestured with his chin.

Max stared over in that direction. "With Colleen? That's Dante."

"What's his story?"

"He works here at Couture." Max cleared his throat. "I think we need to avoid the big-box stores for now. We don't have the inventory, and quite frankly, I think it will cheapen our brand."

"Yeah," Chase said. "What's he do?"

"Dante? He . . . He's an entertainer. So I'm setting up a video shoot with a buddy of mine, Clint. He's also going to be modeling the line. I think you should wear the track suit and the warm-up pants. What do you think?"

"Might as well do the running gear, too," Chase replied, just so that Max knew he was listening. "What type of entertainer? Is he a singer? Comedian?"

"He's a man of many talents." Max slapped him on the back. "I gotta go. I'll see you after the show."

Chase accepted a beer from a passing waiter and glared at the couple. Dante caught his eye and raised an eyebrow at him. Chase would have given anything to mouth the word "mine" at the smug bastard, but he didn't have the right. Not yet. He saluted him with his beer and glared instead. Dante brought the back of Colleen's hand up to his lips and brushed it with a kiss. Chase's vision tinted red until he saw her jerk her hand away and rap her knuckles against his chest.

Good.

Dante didn't make eye contact again.

The interminable show finally ended two beers and a few handfuls of hors d'oeuvres later. Chase pushed his way through the reporters to get closer to Colleen.

"Mrs. Granger?" A female reporter with a thick French accent raised her hand. Chase peeked over at her press badge. Cielo magazine. He shrugged. Never heard of it.

"It's Bryant," Colleen said crisply.

Chase crossed his arms and got ready for the show. For once she was going to go a couple of rounds with someone other than him, and he could enjoy seeing her eyes flash without thinking too hard about the next quip.

"Ms. Bryant," the reporter corrected. "Who were your inspirations for this line?"

"My partner, Anya Litton, and I worked very closely together. We brought in aspects from anime and punk, as well as some whimsical effects."

"Is Ms. Litton still seeing Cesare di Giovanni?"

"No." An amused smile flickered over Colleen's face.

"Are you seeing anyone?"

The smile faded, and she locked gazes with Chase. "No," she said.

He resisted the urge to kiss her senseless in front of all these reporters. So she wasn't seeing that clown Dante. That would make things less complicated.

"What qualifications do you have that made you think you could start your own fashion line?" That question was from a man who wore more hair product than most women. His tag said Vogue. Chase wondered if he could crop-dust the little creep without giving himself away. He moved toward him with intent.

Colleen raised that gorgeous eyebrow of hers and said, "I was encouraged by some friends. Donatella and Jean Paul were especially supportive."

"It doesn't hurt to have all that money from your husband's holdings."

"Money makes the world go round," she tossed out with a fake, carefree laugh.

"You seem to like money."

"Who doesn't? I imagine that's why you're working for *Vogue* instead of trudging through the Middle East doing investigative reporting. Or is there another reason you chose fashion over more 'hard-hitting' stories?" She made finger quotes at him.

The reporter gritted his teeth.

"It's such a bore when people belittle your passions, isn't it?" she followed up. "It's hard to gain respect when all they see is what's on the outside. But in the case of Fierocity, what's outside is fabulous. Tell me, what were your favorites?"

"How the hell did she wind up asking the questions?" the Vogue reporter muttered as Chase walked by him.

A few seconds later, the reporter coughed and moved from the spot.

Chase smiled smugly.

After a couple more interviews, Anya and her bodyguard, a man Max had introduced to him as Clint, entered into the throng of reporters. Anya was still wearing the swirly dress and flashed those hot stockings at the crowd. Amid all the camera flashes and the catcalls for more, the big Russian, Istvahn, inserted himself between the paparazzi and Colleen as she left the runway area.

He had nearly caught up with them when an old guy in a cheap suit stopped them. "The wife and I truly enjoyed the show."

Chase tried to move around Colleen's bodyguard but couldn't get close enough.

"Thank you, Senator," Colleen replied. "I appreciate you being here."

"I'd like to bring her into our session."

Colleen spotted Chase bearing down on her, and put on a tight smile. "I'm sure that can be arranged. But let's discuss that at another time, shall we?" Her inclined head made the senator follow the angle to where Chase was still trying to outmaneuver the Russian, who he was glad had never played pro ball with him.

"Of course. Aren't you Chase Fairwood?" Clemmons came over and shook his hand enthusiastically. "I saw the game that took you out of the league. That was a helluva hit."

Chase made small talk with the senator while Colleen escaped. At least Dante wasn't with her. He sighed and let her go. He'd see her in a few days, and she wouldn't be running away from him again.

CHAPTER 4

Colleen didn't agonize over what to wear tonight. Aside from the fact she had a lending closet full of brand-new designer outfits, her own closet rivaled a department store. She had hand-selected her costume for the dungeon with great attention to detail. The trick was seeing if Chase took the bait and followed her down the rabbit hole into her dungeon, or if he ran scared. She wasn't sure which option she was rooting for. On the one hand, she had been burning up her vibrator just thinking about getting him naked in her dungeon. On the other hand, it was better if he just left for good. Colleen was caught between scaring him off and fucking him silly.

She was leaning toward fucking him silly.

The first Friday of every month, the Hot Spot got its freak on. Instead of club music, the DJ was instructed to play a little bit of everything to gauge the participants' reaction. She touched the earpiece to connect to Istvahn.

"How's the door?"

"We're going to be at capacity." Istvahn's voice was loud in her ear, so she turned down the sound. She wasn't in the club yet.

"Did the VIPs arrive yet?" Colleen tried for nonchalance.

"Fairwood is here, if that's what you're asking."

She made a face. She hated being so obvious. "Thanks."

Her next call was to the bar, where she had them send over a bottle of Johnnie Walker Blue Label with her compliments. She'd be sharing that with him in a few.

After a final check to make sure the dungeon was just as she wanted it, Colleen squared her shoulders.

"It's show time."

Walking into the elevator, she took it up to her special apartment behind the stage at the Hot Spot. She hadn't rented it out tonight, hoping that if Chase spooked and wouldn't go for the dungeon, he'd agree to come back there for a few drinks. She'd bring the dungeon to him. She had a bunch of toys ready to use. One way or another, she planned on getting laid tonight. And it was about damned time, too.

Colleen adjusted her halter dress. It had reminded her of Marilyn Monroe's iconic dress, only instead of white, this one was a wicked shade of red. She had the lipstick made to match the dress and wore her hair wavy and down around her shoulders, just the way Chase liked it. She didn't bother with a bra or underwear. If luck went her way, she wouldn't be in this dress for very long. Her plan was to go big or go home. Chase would be too wound up to even consider stopping. Once they hit the sheets, they could get all the pent-up sexual frustration out and see what shook loose.

Opening the door, Colleen stepped out into the club. In the dim light, no one would be able to see the door close, and it would be impossible to open it without knowing exactly how to trigger the mechanism. Two thrones sat on the stage. Someone tonight would be crowned the King and Queen of Sex.

Putting a sway into her hips to the tune the DJ was playing, "Pour Some Sugar on Me," she walked toward Chase's table. It was half-moon shaped, with wide booth seating. A purple tablecloth pleated in front hid the lower half of his body. He saw her striding toward him and paused with his drink halfway to his mouth.

"I'm glad you made it," she purred.

"Are you wearing a bra?"

"No." She slid into the booth next to him, preening a bit as he fucked her with his eyes. "Why don't you pour us a drink?"

Chase grabbed the bottle and was tilting it when she unbuckled his pants and popped open the button. The scotch shook a little, but he managed to keep it in the glass. "What are you doing?"

"I'm going to stroke your cock in front of all these people. Do you mind?" She didn't give him a chance to answer, just reached in and pulled him out. Even half hard, he was thick. Colleen traced her fingernail over the veins and circled her thumb over the tip.

"Jesus," he breathed, swiveling his head around to see if anyone was watching. A bead of sweat appeared on his forehead. He gasped when she tugged on him.

"Oh, calm down," Colleen said, holding him tight while she pumped him slow. He filled her hand, and the anticipation nearly killed her. "They can't see what I'm doing. The table is too high. In fact, the reason there's a skirt around the table is if I decide to slip to my knees and blow you, no one will know."

"God," he ground out, grabbing the back of her head. "Kiss me."

"No." She pulled back but didn't release him. He was fully erect now, and she reveled in the feel of him in her palm. She locked eyes with him, stroking him long and hard now. She knew her aggression was throwing him, but she got off on the control and vowed to come on stronger. He needed to respect her as a Domme—even if he didn't realize that was what he was doing.

"A few days ago you threatened to turn me into a eunuch if I kissed you. Now you're jerking me off in a dance club?"

"You wanted a second chance," she reminded him, loosening her grip.

He put his hand over hers, encouraging her to continue. "Don't get me wrong. I like it. I'm just wondering what changed. You dodged me at your fashion show. I figured I was on the shit list again."

"Just building up the anticipation. I told you, if you could handle the Hot Spot, you could handle me."

"I'm going to come all over that pretty dress." Chase's teeth were clenched. His hands wouldn't stay still, like he didn't know where to put them.

"No you're not," she said.

His breathing grew more ragged. "In your mouth, then?"

"Not just yet." She stroked her thumb over the tip to capture the glistening drop at the top and licked it off her finger.

"Cock teasing?" he ground out.

"It's only teasing if you don't follow through. I'm testing your limits. Public displays are okay, then; just not too public." Colleen pulled his shirt over his cock. "Don't put that away. I'm going to need that."

He took a hard swallow of his drink.

"I'm not wearing underwear either." She pulled up the skirt of her dress so he could see the swatch of blond hair at the juncture of her thighs.

Tossing her leg over his, Colleen leaned back with her scotch. "You can finger me if you want."

"Is this a trick?" His voice was hoarse, his eyes wild.

"Touch me, Chase." She flicked her tongue over the rim of her glass.

"Let's get out of here," he whispered. "Before I fuck you in this booth in front of everyone."

"We're staying," she said. "I've got things to show you."

"I see them." He rubbed his knuckles against the soft hair before moving them down between her legs. "God, you're soaked."

She was, too. It had been a while since she'd played like this. Chase wasted no time dipping his fingers inside her. Colleen took a deep breath and let out an urgent moan.

Chase's stared deep into her eyes as he slowly pumped his fingers in and out of her.

"I'd like you to make me come," she said, sipping her drink. It wasn't quite phrased like an order. In fact, her voice shook a little. It surprised her how much she wanted this.

"Here? Now? Like this?"

"Just like this." She sighed and spread her legs to give him better access. She remembered them back in Vegas, when any darkened corner was fair game. He'd once gotten her off as he was driving along the Strip, very similarly to how he was doing it now.

Clamping down on his fingers, she hid a gasp in her glass. Chase stopped the wonderful thrusting and was now flicking her swollen clit. It was heavenly to be stroked so intimately in public. She liked the disbelief and heat in his expression. It was about time Chase wasn't so self-confident and assured in her presence.

"I can't believe I'm doing this. What if someone comes over?" His whisper was harsh, but his fingers were so sweet inside her.

"We can let them watch." Colleen grinned over her glass at him.

"Like hell," he growled. "You're mine."

She shivered at his tone. "Mmmm." She arched as he played around her folds and tickled her bud. "Hard limit. Only you and I play."

"Damn right. Very hard."

"I can imagine."

Chase's fingers were as intoxicating as the Scotch. She stared out at the Hot Spot, feeling like the queen of all she surveyed, letting his magic work through her.

"You still with me, baby?" He rubbed faster.

"Yes," she whispered, her voice an octave higher than normal. Her nipples were tight against the silky material of her dress. She wanted very much to climb on top of him.

"You are dripping wet. I can't wait to fuck you."

"You're going to have to. But . . ." She gasped as the pleasure crested. The rush of adrenaline at coming in public was almost as thrilling as the much-needed release. "I'll make sure you enjoy the wait."

She eased his fingers out and smoothed down her skirt, satisfaction humming through her. "Did you like that?"

"Fuck. Yes. No. It was remote."

Colleen cocked her head at him. "What do you mean?"

"You held back. I held back. I want more."

She smiled. "There's more to be had. Now, should I put my lipstick all over your cock or do you want to wait?"

Chase looked around the bar again. "Please."

"Please, Mistress?" she teased.

"Please, Mistress, let me fuck your mouth."

"Very good," she said seriously, and slowly slid to the floor.

See, he can be taught.

Having him give her the honorific made her pussy clench, and she wanted to reward him.

Chase guided his cock into her mouth, and immediately

every muscle in his body locked. "Shit. This is going to be quick."

Colleen moaned in approval and deep-throated him.

"Oh fuck. Son of a bitch. Feels incredible."

She spared him no mercy, sucking him deep in her throat. One of his hands was tangled in her hair. The other was white-knuckled on the seat. The sounds coming out of him were barely coherent. Colleen thought he'd lost the ability to speak English. He came hard, coating her throat as his whole body shook. Colleen finished him off with a few licks and tucked him back in his pants before gracefully sliding back into the seat. She tossed the hair out of her face and stretched languidly. No one was watching them. No one seemed to have noticed or cared what had just happened. Pity.

Chase still trembled, and the hand that reached for his drink wasn't steady. "I couldn't stop. I couldn't last. I . . ."

"Shhh, it's okay, honey." Colleen cuddled up into his side. Chase wrapped his arm around her and kept her close.

"I want you to watch the dance floor and tell me what you see," she said. He smelled so familiar that when she closed her eyes, she was transported back in time to the Las Vegas Strip.

He had been driving a red convertible. The top was down. The night was cool and they had no place else to be. She loved him with all her heart. After they took advantage of the traffic to get each other off, just as they had a few moments ago, Colleen had wrapped her arms around him and it felt like heaven. Nothing had changed.

She loved him with all her heart.

It shook her. She wasn't that girl anymore. She wasn't.

Hell no. Not again.

Colleen wanted the emotional and physical distance, so she eased away from him.

Just hot sex. This can't be permanent.

She was feeling raw and vulnerable, and that just wouldn't do. This was sex. Not love. And she needed to remind herself not to get lost in her own fantasy scene. Chase was not into the lifestyle. They were a time bomb. When this thing between them exploded, Colleen had to keep her heart protected from the shrapnel. She couldn't let him hurt her again. There were no Alfies to rescue her this time.

Needing to get them both back on track, Colleen gestured out into the club. "Look all around the room. If you see what I want you to, I'll give you a surprise."

"Baby, you've given me two already. I'm not sure my heart can take any more."

"Don't worry. I'll give you time to recover in between."

They finished their drinks and were on the second round when Chase asked, "What's in the little rooms off the side? At first I thought they were restrooms, but there's something off."

He didn't miss a trick. Colleen liked how this scene was coming together. "Are you ready for your next surprise?"

"Hell yeah."

"Buckle up."

Chase frowned in confusion, then realized his pants were still undone.

"Come with me." She held out her hand.

"I already did."

"Come again."

"As you wish." He grabbed her hand, and she led him to one of the rooms.

The room smelled of cedar, and the interior was all wood. A cushionless bench faced a window that was currently shuttered closed. When Colleen shut the door and slid the lock, the shutter opened up.

Chase's jaw dropped.

"Like what you see?" Colleen shrugged her shoulders out of the halter top of the dress and pressed herself back against the wall.

Chase fixated on her naked chest. "What are you doing?" he asked.

She grabbed his hands and placed them on her breasts. "I don't have any oil, so you'll just have to pretend."

Without looking, she knew that he was watching a couple making love while covered in oil. Chase's hands were rough as he alternated watching the couple and staring at her. He hauled her away from the wall to sit on the bench. Pulling her onto his lap, he tugged so she sat astride him. Chase plucked at her nipples to the point of pain before soothing them, circling the pad of his thumb over the tight buds.

"I like it when you're a little rough with my nipples." Colleen said, clutching his shoulders for support. Her head was whirling with a passion she thought had been banked by her first orgasm.

"I remember." He captured her nipple in his mouth, sucking hard enough that her head tipped back in bliss. He held her with one strong hand on her back. The other hand massaged her other breast.

"Oh, that's so good," she encouraged, feeling his cock strain against his jeans. Her pulse raced, and flares of need shot straight down to her pussy with each roll of his tongue. "I'm going to soak your pants."

"Don't care," he said, lifting his head up. He attacked the other breast, his teeth grazing over the peak.

Colleen grabbed his hair. "Don't you want to watch?" She was going to dry-hump him until she came if he kept this up.

"Why would I want to watch strangers when I could have these beautiful tits in my face?" He pushed her breasts together so he could suck on both nipples at once.

Colleen lost control and held him there while she rode him to a desperate and wild orgasm, the bulge in his pants providing friction at just the right spot.

"Yeah." He slid his hand under the back of her dress. "Use me to get off." He clutched at her ass while he nipped at her breasts, which were bouncing in his face.

She shuddered against him, feeling like she had been run over by a train. That was not how it was supposed to have gone. He was supposed to watch the show, play with her breasts a bit, and that was it. Colleen was dangerously losing control over her own scenario. They were going to fuck next time. She could feel it in the set of his body. In the next private space, this skirt was going up to her ears and he was going to bang the shit out of her.

Colleen sighed and almost pulled his cock out, but that would ruin all her plans. He needed to be the one out of control, not her. So instead she slid off him and fixed her dress.

"Seen enough?" she asked over her shoulder.

"Hardly—you got dressed again. Let's get out of here."

"I thought you wanted a membership to Couture." She crossed her arms over her chest.

"My dick is so hard right now, all I want is to dip it in that hot, wet pussy and lose myself for a few hours."

"I want that, too." Colleen grabbed his hand. "But you have to trust me that there is more that you need to see and experience before that can happen."

He blew out a hard sigh. "It's your circus."

"You have no idea," she said, and they went back to the table. Colleen motioned for the waiter to bring over a pitcher of water, and she poured them both two tall glasses.

"I like your surprises," he said, reaching down to hold her hand again.

"You ain't seen nothing yet," she told him.

While she tried to get her harried senses under control, the party was in full swing. She leaned her cheek against his shoulder while he stroked her knuckles with his thumb. The strippers, both male and female, came out and were dancing naked in cages. Some patrons followed suit. She toggled on her earpiece.

"Micah, take note of the dancers for the list."

"I'm on it. Why don't you take the night off? I can handle managing the crowd."

Colleen opened her mouth to protest, but Anya's words about her being a control freak drifted back to her. "Sounds great," she said. "Let's meet tomorrow and go over the information." She couldn't totally let it go, but she could free up her evening to devote to Chase.

"What's that all about?" he asked. "You're not going to kick them out, are you? They're just having a good time. Unless you're worried about indecency charges?"

Colleen gave a small laugh. "This is private property. What happens in Couture stays in Couture."

"Like Vegas," he said.

"Not exactly, but you're close." Too close, as it turned out.

Chase grabbed her chin, turning it so she was looking at him instead of the strippers. "So when do I get to bury myself in you and kiss you senseless?"

"Soon," she promised. "Right now I need you to hold on, because things are about to get a little kinky."

A naked man was brought out, bent over a sawhorse on wheels.

"Free spankings," a woman dressed in black leather shouted. "The line forms over here."

"I'm not spanking him," Chase said as a few people milled over to slap the man.

"What about her?" Colleen pointed when a woman, similarly posed, was wheeled out with a man in leather.

"Isn't this a little dangerous?" Chase asked. "What if some drunk wants to do more than spank her?"

"Her Dom is there to protect her. As is his Domme."

"Dom?" Chase blinked. "Dominant? Dominatrix? Like what you were doing in Vegas?"

Colleen took a deep breath. *Here goes nothing.* "What I'm still doing," she said. "Watch the spankings. The Dom is there for control. The pleasure is for the sub and the people spanking him or her."

"What do you mean, you're still doing it?"

"This is another part of my organization. I create scenes like this for select people."

Chase whipped his head back to her. "You're not wheeling me out there for free whacks."

"What about in private?" she murmured.

"I'm not into pain," he said. "Got my fill of that with this." He rubbed his knee.

A slight wave of disappointment hit her, but she knew he was new to the lifestyle. She'd put the spanking down as a hard limit for now. Maybe later, after they got used to fooling around, she'd take him right up to that limit and see if he'd step over the line.

After the spankings, there were requests for volunteers.

"No fucking way," Chase told her.

"I heard you the first time." Colleen smiled. "But I have to know, is your dick still hard?"

He smirked. "Yeah."

"Good. You want to dance?"

"No. I want to fuck you. I've seen enough. I get it. The Hot Spot gets a little kinky. Who cares?"

"All right," Colleen said. "I think you're ready for the next step."

"Is the next step feeling that sweet pussy grip my cock?"

"Eventually," she said, and led him by the hand to the elevators.

CHAPTER 5

C hase pushed her up against the wall of the elevator and claimed the kiss he had been waiting for. He had just gripped her ass when the doors opened.

"Damn, short trip. Let's ride this a couple of times." He looked for a button to press, but there weren't any.

"Follow me," Colleen said, and walked out into a darkened hallway.

Chase tore his gaze away from her luscious ass and took in his surroundings. "What is this place?"

Stylized flames on the wall gave off the only illumination. Up ahead he heard a scream. Grabbing Colleen's arm, he shoved her behind him. If some psycho came at them, they'd have to go through him first.

"Chase," she said, "relax."

The scream faded into sobs.

Adrenaline surged through him as he sought out the danger. The hallway opened to a wider section. Black curtains sealed off a few alcoves. The noise level grew, and the background hum of voices allowed him to push back the fight-or-flight response pounding in his veins. It was just another club, a little darker and a little raunchier than the one they'd just left. Unlike the Hot Spot, this place didn't have any music, but there were a few bars scattered around the cavernous room. People were dressed in all sorts of costumes. He could see a cowboy wearing only chaps. Acrobats dangled naked from the ceiling, and a bare-chested woman with a python around her neck strolled around.

"Is this a carnival, or is every night Halloween?"

"This," Colleen said, whirling around to face him, "is Club Inferno."

"It is pretty hot," he admitted, running his hand through his hair. "I was hoping we were going someplace a little more private."

Like her bedroom, where they could lock themselves in for a few days, order some room service, and get to know each other all over again.

"We are." She turned back around and walked away from him. He wanted to lick down the low back of her dress, so he hurried to catch up to her.

"Mistress," a naked man acknowledged Colleen. Well, he wasn't totally naked. He wore a dog collar and a leather mask.

"What the serious fuck, Colleen?" Chase said after the man dropped to his knees.

Colleen passed by without acknowledging the man. "Club Inferno is a series of dungeons and sexual playgrounds literally beneath Couture. Up there"—she pointed—"it's a fashion resort. Down here is where the real action is."

"Dungeons?" He gave a quick search around to see if there were medieval torture chambers. He did see a woman strapped down on a table with another man using a leather flail on her breasts. And that wasn't the most sexual thing down here. There was one guy going down on a chick who was blowing another guy while a small crowd cheered them on. Chase whirled and saw two clowns in makeup that would give anyone nightmares chasing two screaming women.

"Is your head going to explode?" Colleen said, dragging him into a private room.

"There are people having sex out there—in public." Chase craned his neck out the door before Colleen pushed him inside and locked them in. That was more like it. But when he reached for her, she had moved into the middle of the room.

It took him a minute to realize they were standing in his old locker room at training camp. The details were perfect, down to the dent in the big hot tub in the corner. Hanging up was his old uniform. Stubbing his foot on the bench as he rushed over, he pulled it out. Was he dreaming all of this? Had she spiked his scotch?

"I'll be right back," Colleen murmured, pausing to fondle his cock on her way out. "Suit up."

It perked right back up, but his other head was still reeling.

Out of habit, or maybe it was muscle memory, Chase stripped off his clothes and put on his uniform, wincing as he bent his knee to put on his cleats. His heart was tripping in excitement. If he closed his eyes, he could picture himself getting ready to take the field. His hand itched for the football. He thrust to his feet, and his knee buckled.

"Shit." He sank back down on the bench and held his head until the pain ebbed to a dull throb. Standing up more gingerly, the way he had been taught in physical therapy, Chase was able to straighten and walk around the room.

Stupid limp. The physical therapist had said that it might go away, but not to be disappointed if it didn't.

In the bathroom mirror, Chase stared at his reflection. He wasn't expecting to see the pain reflected in his eyes—pain that had nothing to do with his stupid knee. The roaring in his ears wasn't the crowd at the stadium or even from the freaks outside. The room was silent. That and the fact that he was in an NFL uniform again were the only hints that this was a fantasy.

Colleen came back into the room dressed in his team's cheerleading outfit. "I figured if you want to fuck a cheerleader, we can do it here fast and quick." She tilted up her skirt and wiggled her bare ass at him. "Then get it on again in the hot tub."

Chase swallowed, his cock twitching. "I'm still not sure what this is all about." Where was she going with all of this? Was she going to tease him and then slap the shit out of him? Was that what got her off nowadays?

Colleen leaned against the lockers with one foot on the bench. He watched, transfixed, as she began to play with her pussy. Those blond curls tempted him, and he stepped closer to see the pretty pink flesh between her thighs. "What's confusing you?" Colleen said in a husky voice.

If his knee hadn't been killing him, he might have dropped to his knees and helped her out.

"This place." He gestured with his helmet. "These outfits. What are you running down here?"

"Sexual fantasy fulfillment," she said, speeding up her fingers enough that he could hear the wetness as she stroked herself. "When I told you Couture was many things to different people, well, this is one side that few members get a chance to see. Any kink you want can be explored. I've got rope specialists, dominants and submissives . . . you name it."

"So this is like Miranda's Midnight House of Pain?" He didn't like the thought that she was this wild and free with just anyone.

"On a much grander and larger scale. I am the head

mistress. These are my dungeons, and I control everything that goes on here."

"You're a pimp?"

Colleen stopped masturbating and glared at him. "I'm a sex instructor."

"I don't need any instruction." A cold pit was forming in his stomach. He tossed his helmet on the floor. This was a joke to her. A game.

Shaking her head, Colleen said, "I know you don't. You aren't one of my clients. We're here to have some mind-blowing sex. I thought that's what you wanted."

Chase heard the aggravation in her voice, and he fed it back to her. "It was. I figured we'd go back to your place—your place being a bedroom, not a locker room—and fuck like normal people."

"Normal people?" Colleen's voice rose, but he didn't care. He tore off his team jersey, accurate down to the stitching, and kicked off his cleats.

"I don't need all this fancy shit."

"I thought this would be fun," she said in a small voice. "I thought it would tie together some loose ends we have."

"I don't have any loose ends. This place is seriously freaking me out." He pulled off the uniform pants. "The screaming and all the naked bodies . . ."

"Since when are you a prude?" She crossed her arms over her chest.

He started to get dressed. "In Vegas you did this to make money. You can buy a small island. Why are you still doing this?"

"I like it." She had no right staring at him like that, like he had three heads. She was the one dressed up like a cheerleader.

"Do you get paid to have sex with people?" He paused in putting on his shirt as a sick feeling passed over him. Maybe

Granger had convinced her that she had to perform for her lovers. Perhaps he'd even rented her out to his friends.

"I'm not a whore." She got in his face, but instead of grabbing her for a kiss he backed off.

"What do you call it?"

"I give people a place to act out their desires. I help people with their sex lives. I fuck who I want. Up until five minutes ago, it was you."

"Yeah, well, I'm out of here." Chase took another step away from her. "I don't want to be spanked or tortured or any of that shit. If I wanted to bang a cheerleader in my locker room, I could have done that. Thanks for outlining that I can't do it anymore."

The last sentence hung in the air between them. He didn't want to see the concern on her pretty face or the pity in her eyes, so he turned his back on her.

This sucks.

He took a deep breath, trying to get back to the place where he was going to make up for the ten years they'd been apart. But it was gone. The sick feeling in his gut sat there like a bowling ball. He had come once tonight, and the urgency was gone.

Damn her. I could have gone all night if she hadn't pulled this shit.

"I didn't set up this scene to make you feel bad. Chase, it's just playacting. It would have been hot sex. I wasn't going to put you in spandex and a ball gag and parade you around the dungeon shouting 'Bring out the gimp.'" She shook his shoulder lightly.

"This isn't you," he said, turning to grab her arms. "Did Granger make you do this for him?"

"Chase, this *is* me. It's always been me. And I'm not discussing my sex life with Alfie with you. It's none of your business. You weren't a virgin when we met and you haven't been one since. This shouldn't be as shocking as you're making it out to be."

He shuddered. "You can't tell me it wasn't about the money between the two of you. You could have had any guy you wanted. If Granger wasn't a multibillionaire—if he was just some old fart in a retirement home—you'd never have married him."

She pulled away from him, rubbing away his touch. "Yeah, and if I wasn't blond with big tits, you never would have looked twice at me."

"That's different."

"Is it, Chase? If we'd met in the casino and I'd been wearing a dowdy suit and was flat-chested, would you have asked me to escort you around the shops? If I'd had gray hair and wore it in a bun and my glasses were slipping down my big nose, would you have come back every day for a week just to be with me?"

Chase shook his head. "You're twisting this all back on me. I didn't marry for money."

Colleen reacted as if he'd slapped her. "Neither did I. You shouldn't believe everything you read in the tabloids."

"You would have married him if he wasn't a billionaire?" Chase folded his arms and glared at her.

"If the situation had been the same, yes."

Now it was Chase's turn to reel back. "If I hadn't been in bed with those skanks, you never would have married Granger?"

"That's right," Colleen said. "I would have told Alfie that I was in a committed relationship with a man I—" She broke off and turned away. "This was a mistake. I tried telling you that."

"Finish that thought," Chase whispered. He would saw off his legs to hear her say she loved him.

But Colleen only blew out a sigh. "I tried telling *myself* that this was a mistake."

She had no idea what she was doing to him.

Hell, he had no idea.

"I should go," he said, but he couldn't force his feet to move. This can't be going down like this. Not an hour ago, she'd had his dick in his mouth. He could still smell her on his fingers. If he could just convince her that he didn't need all this stuff, maybe they could get back to that place. She had thrown him into a maelstrom with the uniform. It felt like a kick in the junk. Part of him wasn't sure that she didn't mean it as a cruel trick. And then, just now—she said she wouldn't have married the Texas billionaire if they had been together. More mind games?

"I'd appreciate your discretion about Club Inferno. I broke my own rules allowing you to come down here. You have the power to ruin this experience for a lot of people. Please don't." Her jaw was set, but he could see a slight tremor in her chin.

"I'm not saying anything. I'm just going to pretend this never happened." Chase shook his head to clear it. That was the best solution. Start over and never come back down here again. It hadn't been at all bad, but he'd show her she didn't need to get dressed up for him to want her. Next time they could go back to his place, maybe get drunk and have some sloppy reunion sex. They'd talk about Granger once it wasn't so raw between them.

"Thank you," she said quietly. He saw the shimmer of tears, but he didn't know what to do. He needed to get out of the locker room and have some time to think. But he couldn't leave her, not like this.

"At least now I know why Max made me get all those tests before I started modeling," Chase said, trying to lighten the mood. "I thought it was overkill."

"We take the safety of our members very seriously," she said stiffly.

He sighed. "I don't want to end the night like this. Can we get out of here?"

Colleen shook her head. "No. And this time stay away from me. You and I have no future. We're too different. This is my world. I am a pro Domme. I like fulfilling fantasies and helping people enjoy their sex lives."

"This is too much for me right now. I need some time to think."

"I know," she said sadly. "I think you should leave." She touched her ear. "Istvahn, please escort Mr. Fairwood off property."

"I can find my own way out." Chase didn't like the idea of being manhandled by her bodyguard.

"It's for our safety as well as yours."

There was a discreet knock on the door.

"Enter," Colleen said.

Istvahn, who must have been close by, nodded to Chase. He didn't look twice at his boss dressed up like a wet dream. "Let's go."

A flare of panic reached through his haze of confusion as Chase realized this wasn't fuck off. It was fuck off and die.

"Colleen, we can work this out."

"You can stay at Couture for Max's sake. I won't be seeing you again, and the dungeon areas are off-limits to you."

He would have stayed and argued, but Istvahn put him in an armlock and nearly frog-marched him out of the room.

The door closed on her, and the last glimpse he had of her in that short cheerleading outfit was burned into his mind. What the hell had he just done?

Asshole.

CHAPTER 6

"I can't believe you're going to hide up here while Max has his first show," Colleen's sister, Mallory, said. She stood in the doorway of Colleen's office with her arms crossed over her chest. She was wearing an Ann Taylor outfit, which was a step up from her jeans and T-shirts—when she wasn't in her medical scrubs.

"You should try some new pieces from Stella McCartney. Have Nefertiti give you the keys to the lending closet."

"Don't change the subject."

Colleen took a sip of her diet cola and raised an eyebrow. "Do I stalk you at your job and tell you that your triage is in the wrong order?"

Mallory came in and flopped down in the seat across from Colleen's desk. "I love it when you use words you learned from George Clooney on *ER*."

"Could be worse. I could be quoting House. He's a cranky bastard." Colleen checked out her manicure and hoped Mallory would take the hint and go away.

"So are you."

"Fine. If you want to go to your husband's first clothing

launch dressed in off-the-rack clothes, be my guest." Colleen watched her ploy almost work as Mallory twitched, running a hand down the pretty new clothes she must have bought especially for the occasion.

"Nice try," Mallory said. "It's a sportswear line, not haute couture. No one is going to care what I'm wearing."

"Somebody always notices." Colleen said. She had been on *Fashion Emergency* enough times to have a dartboard with all the hosts' faces on it.

Mallory said nothing.

Colleen stared at her computer screen, not seeing or caring about next week's staff development programming. "I'm not hiding," she said to break the silence and the power of Mallory's glare. "I'm busy."

"You own the freakin' place. You can carve out a few hours if you really want to. This means a lot to Max." And then Mallory played her trump card. "It means a lot to me."

Colleen sighed. "That was low."

"No, low would have been if I'd told you that I deliberately didn't tell Mom about the show so you wouldn't have to put her and Dad up here for the week."

"I would have booked them a suite at the Waldorf-Astoria in Manhattan and sent a limo to ferry them back and forth." Colleen repressed a shudder.

"I don't know what's going on between you and Chase—"

And thank God for that.

"Nothing is going on." Colleen had had a lot of time to think about it—even though she didn't want to. It had been a disaster from the moment she walked into the dungeon. She had come on too strong. If he had been a new member of Club Inferno, she would have eased him into the lifestyle. But because they had a past, she'd plowed into him like a horny Mack truck. It had never occurred to her that he'd be turned off by the slightest hint of kink. Unfortunately, that was as close to vanilla sex as she came nowadays. Truth was, she'd fucked up. She should have stuck to her instincts and kept Chase at arm's length.

"It would mean a lot to me if you supported my husband. Just having you there is a guarantee that the press will give this event some space."

Colleen liked Max. She even thought the sportswear line he had designed was damned good. But she'd spent the last two weeks dodging Chase as he met with Max to strategize how to launch the line. It would be hard to avoid seeing Chase when they were in the same room, especially if he was on the stage. Although he'd be so busy she probably could slip in and out. Enough to give Max the exposure he needed but be back in her office—or, better yet, the dungeon—before Chase was off the runway.

"It's not like I'm asking you to wear a few pieces. Although you'd rock his sports top and yoga pants." Mallory made an hourglass with her hands.

"I'm not going to be photographed in stretch pants and a bra by National Geographic or whoever the fuck is out there." That was all Colleen needed. She could see the headlines: "Aging Heiress Gives Up Haute Couture for Comfort."

"It's Sports Illustrated."

"Really?" Colleen was impressed.

"Chase is giving them an interview."

"That would do it." Chase was an asset in this case. She hoped he wouldn't say anything about Club Inferno, but she was pretty sure he wouldn't. He wasn't the vindictive type, but more important, he'd be too embarrassed to admit he'd been fooling around in a sex dungeon.

Damn it.

"So you'll go?" Mallory grinned.

This was the first time Sports Illustrated had accepted an invitation to Couture. Colleen had been angling to get them interested in some swimwear for their annual swimsuit edition. If they liked Max's line, they might be more inclined to come back the next time they did a bikini show.

Colleen tapped her pen on her desk, weighing the pros and cons. "You're not going to leave me alone until I make an appearance, are you?"

"I'm prepared to drag you by the hair kicking and screaming if I have to."

Colleen was pretty sure she could take her younger sister in a fight, but Mallory's husband was a black belt. "Fine," she grumped. "I can't stay the whole time, though."

"Thank you." Mallory came around the side of the desk and gave her a hug.

"Don't mess up my hair," Colleen grumbled.

Colleen waited until the last minute to enter the auditorium. She knew the models would be backstage by now, minimizing the chance she'd have to make small talk with her former lover. Slipping into a seat next to Anya and Nefertiti, Colleen pretended she didn't see the five-dollar bill Anya forked over to Nefertiti, who whispered, "Told you."

"I'm only here for Max," Colleen said.

"Sure you are," Nefertiti said.

Istvahn took up position behind them but wisely stayed out of the discussion.

The lights dimmed, and then in the background snippets of sports announcers' commentary filled the air. Clint came out first. He was shirtless and wearing the warm-up pants that Max had designed. Not only was Clint one of her Doms, he was marrying Anya. God help him. He had stripped for a few years to make enough money to buy his tequila bar, but he still stuck around Club Inferno to take naughty videos of consenting adults engaged in pleasure.

Leaping into a flying side kick and landing gracefully on the balls of his feet, Clint paused dramatically for the cameras. He winked at Anya and went into a series of high kicks and back kicks.

Jana, feeling much better after her bout with discount sushi, was dressed like a referee. While the cameras flashed, she announced the highlights of the design.

"Clint is wearing treated silk pants designed with wicking properties to keep you cool as you go through your paces."

Anya catcalled when he did a handstand. Rotating his body, Clint walked all the way offstage on his hands.

"Show-off," Colleen teased Anya.

"If you got it . . ." She shrugged.

Max came out next, and Colleen heard Mallory hooting at him from the front row.

"Max is wearing a wool-cotton blend. The drape adds to your silhouette. It's reversible and can be worn alone or as a layer." Jana blew her referee's whistle, and Max turned, unzipped the hoodie, and shrugged it off.

"It helps he's not ugly," Nefertiti said. "Those are some serious guns."

Anya whistled at him through her teeth.

"A little dignity, ladies," Colleen said, feeling the tight band in her chest ease. She had been hiding in her office since that disastrous night in the dungeon. It was time to get over it already.

"Max's tank top is designed to add protection and padding for martial arts sparring. The lightweight material adds a layer of defense without the bulk."

As Max left the stage, a montage of plays made by Chase over the years appeared on the screen above the stage.

"Chase Fairwood with a big sack. Boom! Wind that up, Phil. Let's see that again. Wham! He should work for Amtrak. The train is coming through."

A hiss of steam hazed the entrance to the stage, outlining Chase in a shadow. Colleen had thought she was prepared to see him again, but the burn of humiliation flared. It didn't help that his former teammates were in the front row. They stood up and roared for him. Flashes went crazy when he stepped out wearing only boxing shorts, his hands taped up. Jana droned something about double stitching, but the world stopped for Colleen. He posed in a fighting stance, his wide back exposed to her.

"Breathe," Anya said in her ear.

Colleen forced herself to inhale normally. She shot Anya a dirty look, and when her gaze returned to Chase, he was staring right at her. Colleen hadn't expected to feel that intensity again, hadn't expected him to ever meet her eyes. But he didn't glance away. Butterflies tickled in her stomach and flew lower when she read the raw hunger in his gaze. That was also unexpected; she'd been waiting for disgust or contempt. The sweet burn of lust as he devoured her with his eyes, like he wanted to claim her in front of all these people, awoke a trickle of desire. Colleen swallowed hard.

The son of a bitch blew her a kiss, and her face flamed. Attention swiveled to her. She kept her face devoid of expression as the flashbulbs blinded her for a moment. When her vision cleared, Chase was shadow-boxing his way off the stage.

"Well, well, well, someone's been holding out on us," Nefertiti drawled.

"He's just being an asshole." Colleen forced a lightness in her voice that she was far from feeling. Her heart still hammered as though she were a silly teenager experiencing her first crush. "That was a sarcastic kiss."

"Not from where I was sitting. It looked like he wanted to gobble you up," Anya said.

"The air sizzled," Nefertiti added.

Colleen snorted. "That's a load of bullshit."

"Denial ain't just a river in Egypt," Nefertiti muttered to Anya, but still loud enough for Colleen to hear.

The second pass for all the models featured equal amounts of beefcake and flashy fitness moves. When it was over, Colleen stood to give Max a standing ovation, then turned to Istvahn.

"Stay here with Anya and Nefertiti. I'm going down to the dungeon."

He nodded and blocked for her while she snuck out the back.

"Ms. Bryant!" One reporter had managed to get through the pack. She had to give him props for outmaneuvering Istvahn, so she paused. His badge said he was with Pierre, a French men's magazine.

"*Bonjour*," she said, repressing a sigh.

"Are you dating Chase Fairwood?"

"No," she said, flicking a glance toward the stage, where Chase was surrounded by his buddies. They were thumping him on the back and jeering him good-naturedly. He was searching for something or someone, craning his neck.

Colleen kept walking. Was she imagining feeling Chase's determined stare on her back?

The reporter scurried ahead of her, blocking her escape. "You have a history with him. Weren't you dating a decade ago?"

"We were kids," Colleen said, distracting him with a hand on his arm. "What did you think of the show?"

The reporter glanced down at her hand and then followed it up to her face. "Uh, it was great." He met her smile with one of his own.

She gave his arm a slight squeeze. "I can get you an interview with the designer. Max is my brother-in-law."

"Thanks." He cleared his throat. "You wouldn't be free for dinner tonight, would you?"

Chase was heading over to them, a determined set to his jaw.

Oh, hell no.

"That sounds fabulous," she lied, flashing the reporter a bright smile. "Why don't you meet me at Shira's on the third floor around seven?"

"Wow, yes. *Bien sûr*," he said, reverting to his native language in excitement.

"*À bientôt.*" She kissed the air by his cheek, and booked like hell.

"Colleen," Chase called.

She pretended not to hear and dashed through the door. Pressing against it so it closed quickly, she got it locked behind her just as Chase reached it. She felt the door rattle as he tried to open it. Colleen leaned her head back in relief when he knocked. There was no way in hell she was going to answer that. The Domme part of her was appalled that she'd fled the scene, but the more practical side knew that meeting with Chase after their last encounter shouldn't be done in front of a reporter. Straightening, she hurried down the hall and into the dungeon.

The Doms had set up a party for Max, with champagne on ice and tables filled with shrimp cocktail and bites of chicken and beef. Ropes were coiled up as decorations as a nod to Max's dungeon specialty.

"Those better not be part of his Kinbaku rigs." Colleen took a glass of champagne from a topless sub. Noting that her eyes were downcast, Colleen nodded in approval.

"I don't have a death wish," Micah, who was in charge of the dungeon today, retorted. He indicated that she should sit. A line of male submissives on their hands and knees were acting like benches. She sat delicately on one. Her spine relaxed when Micah handed her a small plate of hors d'oeuvres, bowing to her. Resting the plate on her sub's lower back, she stroked her fingers through the man's lovely black hair while she sipped champagne.

"What's your name, slave?" she asked.

"Jake, Mistress."

"Who do you belong to?"

"I am Master Dante's."

That figured. He had a line of well-behaved slaves. Not to mention that he claimed all of the dungeon's unattached male submissives. "Perhaps I'll ask him to give you to me."

"That would please me, Mistress."

Colleen nodded again, thoughtfully this time. "What else pleases you?"

She felt the tremor through him when she pulled his hair, yanking his head up sharply.

"Anything you wish."

"Good answer," she said, releasing him. She'd talk to Dante about letting her borrow Jake. It was time that she started seeing to her own physical needs. The disaster with Chase was proof that she couldn't take a lover outside of the lifestyle, and this pulse-pounding, panty-dropping lust she felt for Chase every time they looked at each other was probably a result of her denying herself sexually.

Dante was going to make her work for Jake, though. Colleen caressed the sub's lower back; it wasn't as powerful or wide as Chase's, but then again, Jake hadn't been a defensive tackle.

After his whipping Dante had been more respectful, but to her disappointment he never came back for more. Whipping the practice dummy kept her skills sharp, but it had been exhilarating to let loose on Dante.

Colleen was finishing up her shrimp when Mallory and Max led an entourage through Club Inferno—minus Chase, who by her order was barred from entering. Anya came up to her.

"You tore out of there like your ass was on fire."

"I had things to do." She stroked her nails through the sub's hair.

Anya tracked the movement and raised an eyebrow. "Good for you. It's about damn time."

Nefertiti came over with a plate filled high with shrimp. "I need to sit down." Nefertiti snapped her fingers and one of the men across from Colleen scuttled over to her.

"Are you sure about that?" Colleen nodded at the plate.

"I'm going to risk it. I'm suddenly ravenous."

Istvahn grabbed her arm before she could sit on the sub, and settled her into a chair that he had brought over. She shrugged and sank into it. Anya remained standing. The sub crawled back over to someone else.

"Mr. Fairwood is requesting entrance," Istvahn said.

"I think you should let him in. He worked really hard," Anya said.

Nefertiti nodded, her mouth full of shrimp.

Now that Colleen had a plan, she really didn't care if Chase came into Club Inferno—just as long as she wasn't in it at the same time.

She flagged down Micah. "Where's Dante?"

"He's in a private session."

Colleen scowled. "Figures. Have him come see me when he's done." She stood up, leaving her plate and glass on Jake's back. "You can admit Chase into Inferno," she said over her shoulder to Istvahn. "I'll be in my private dungeon. The only person who may disturb me is Dante."

"Where's the fun in that?" Anya complained.

It took only a half hour before Dante was knocking at her door. Colleen let him in but ignored him while she finished the scene for her appointment tomorrow. Her clients were in a committed relationship and wanted an introduction to BDSM.

"How about you lie on the bed and we test out those handcuffs?" Dante stroked his finger around the inside of the cuff attached to the bedpost. "Fleece lined?"

Colleen almost laughed at his sneer. "Don't fuck up my scene. I've got clients coming tomorrow afternoon for their first lesson in bondage."

"You could have at least started with silk scarves." Dante sniffed in disapproval.

"Not that it's any of your business, but we'll be doing some scarf play before the handcuffs. I'm going to give them a little taste of everything, enough to whet their appetites for deeper experiences. They bought the six month program."

"Sounds like fun." Dante whistled. "But not cheap."

"Never cheap." Colleen motioned for him to sit in the wide armchair.

"Are you going to join me?" He patted his lap. "Just lie down across my knees."

Colleen admired his determination. She put a booted foot on his thigh and leaned down enough that the stiletto point pushed into his leg a bit. "I want to ask a favor."

Stroking the leather of her boot, he said idly, "I'm listening."

"I want use of Jake."

"Who's Jake?" Dante encircled her ankle with his hand and pulled her closer.

Colleen shifted her weight so it went on that narrow heel, pushing into his thigh. He held up his hands in surrender. She eased back on the pressure.

"One of the benches out in the club. Nice ass. Long black hair."

"Ah yes. How did you meet him?"

"I was sitting on him at the time."

"He propositioned you?" Dante's face grew grim. "I'll see him punished for that."

"I did the propositioning. He acquiesced that a relationship would be agreeable."

Dante smirked. "I bet. So how long do you want him for?"

"Let's try a month. Maybe longer if I like him. Exclusively."

"I'm afraid I can't do that." Dante gently removed her leg from his. "None of my subs want monogamy. You could have him a few nights a week, but he has other duties that he performs for me."

Well, that sucked. Colleen didn't want to share. "That's too bad," she said, eyeing Dante. He had something else up his sleeve. She just had to give him the rope to hang himself with.

"Is that a deal breaker?" Dante stood up. Colleen decided not to step back to give him room. In her boots she was a few inches taller than him, and she liked that he had to glance up at her.

She crossed her arms under her corset and nodded.

Dante's gaze lingered on her cleavage, as she knew it would. "Perhaps I can be of assistance," he said.

"I need a sex slave, Dante. You don't take orders very well."

"Hear me out," he said.

This ought to be good. Colleen indicated with a nod that he should continue. He rested his hand on her hip, and for the moment she let him keep it there. She found it strange that there wasn't any tickling in her nether regions when she was this close to Dante. No desire to shove him back on that chair and ride him until they were both hoarse from screaming. She was entertained, though. Maybe that could be enough.

"I'd like to learn to be a switch."

Colleen almost reached for her eyebrows to stop them from flying off the top of her head.

"But I'd like you to switch for me, too," he added in the next breath.

Biting her tongue to keep from laughing, she fought to remain poised. Dante wanted to be dominated, but only if he could dominate her in turn. It wasn't unheard of. A lot of Dommes switched to submissive depending on their lovers. But Colleen wasn't a switch. She was a top and had only been submissive to one man.

Colleen couldn't give away that gift of control to just anyone. It would mar Alfie's memory if she submitted to a man just to get laid. Dante had charisma and power. He was a damned good Dom. His subs were the best in the club—which was why Colleen was trying to pilfer one. But Alfie *was* power.

His illness had sometimes limited what they could do in the bedroom. So he told her exactly how she could please him. How to sit. How to offer herself to him. What to do and when. It was a relief to know he would guide her through their lovemaking and take care of her needs both in and out of the bedroom. It had been a blessing to let go, to stop thinking and just feel. Alfie had been in control. He handled everything. All she had to do was follow orders and orgasm when he allowed it. The first time he dominated her, Colleen came until she thought she would go blind. It was addicting stuff. But now it was gone, and she didn't want to give that control to anyone else. She wasn't that twenty-year-old girl searching for direction and guidance. It was her turn to direct and guide.

"Why do you want to bottom?" Colleen asked. Maybe Dante needed to let go as well. He certainly worked hard enough around here.

"I'm bored."

Well, that was a thrilling admission. Colleen controlled her sigh and resisted telling him to go read a book or something. Luckily, he continued to talk on and didn't notice her hesitation.

"I want someone to take care of me for a change. Do you think that's selfish?"

No, she didn't. So she shook her head. "I'm honored that you trust me enough to do that for you." It was certainly more than the senator was willing to give her.

"So when do you want to start?" Dante leaned in to kiss her.

For a moment she almost let him. But she turned and stepped away, leaving him hanging. She didn't want to have sex with him. But she could still dominate Dante. At least she'd be able to fill that need for him.

Alfie had once asked the same thing from her. He had known he was dying, but he didn't tell anyone. Colleen found out after his death that his doctor had told him he had about a year left to live.

But she hadn't known any of that. She'd just figured that her husband wanted to switch things up in the bedroom. So she'd let Alfie guide her through domination and control, instilling in her the belief that it was the dominant's duty to see to the care of his slave. When she mastered his lessons to his satisfaction, he had her switch back to submissive. But it hadn't been the same. After feeling the rush of being a Domme, it was hard to be content as a sub.

During that time, Alfie had made her CEO of all his hotel properties, knowing that his family would fight her on the inheritance after his death. Then in between watching her get herself off on various tools and devices, having her walk around in his presence naked—or, if she was being punished, clipping clothespins on her body—he taught her how to run those businesses. It didn't hurt that he had world-class employees who knew their jobs and were loyal to him. Alfie had had a way of bringing that out in people. Just as he'd had a way of bringing out the submissive side that she no longer had. The thought of kneeling at Dante's feet with a collar and a leash turned her stomach a bit. However, if Dante was at her feet, she could work with that.

"I'll train you to be a switch," she said. "But I remain a top."

He took her in his arms. "No deal."

Colleen shook him off before he could complete the clinch. "The choice is, of course, yours. If Jake changes his mind about monogamy . . ."

"He won't," Dante bit out.

"Neither will I. You have my permission to leave." She took precisely one step back and indicated the door with a flourish of her arm.

"You're making a mistake," he said over his shoulder.

"I make them all the time." Colleen forced a note of gaiety into her voice. But the slam of the door almost brought her to tears.

CHAPTER 7

Chase wondered if it was all right to sport wood in Club Inferno—without being taken for a participant. There was skin everywhere. The servers were topless, both men and women. They had nipple clamps attached to a chain. If you wanted a drink, you tugged them over. If you wanted more than a drink, they sank to their knees. This place was off the hook.

And yet he found himself hoping to catch a glimpse of Colleen. He didn't think she'd be in her little cheerleading outfit, but it bothered him that she might be behind closed doors with someone else. It bothered him a lot. It reminded him of how fast she'd moved on after their last fight ten years ago. If she got married again . . . Chase broke out in a cold sweat. A part of him knew he was being ridiculous, but the caveman part wanted to get his club and go hunting for his woman. They'd had a stupid fight. He'd been taken aback, and instead of just thinking with his little head, because Colleen meant a lot more to him than a quick fuck in a fantasy sex room, he'd done the noble thing and left to give them some space.

Having space sucked. He was over it as soon as he hit the highway and spent the rest of the drive home cursing himself for being a grade-A jackass. So what if she liked sex a little kinky? As long as she saved it for him, who really gave a fuck if she wanted to be banged wearing a cheerleader outfit? It wasn't as if she was walking around with her tits on a leash. She owned the place. Chase averted his gawking stare from a few male slaves who were pretending to be horses. Their riders steered them with a bridle and a riding quirt to a starting line marked with tape on the floor.

To each his own, right?

As long as she didn't expect him to giddyup, they wouldn't have a problem. Chase took a beer from a redhead with great knockers. Not that he was looking—much. He shifted so his jacket covered the growing bulge in his pants. Chase had to hand it to Colleen. She didn't do things half-assed. He never would have guessed that she had a thriving sex club down below Couture. The shit that was going down here made the Hot Spot's spankings seem tame.

"What did you think of your first time on the runway?" Anya sidled up and asked him.

He turned to face her. She was wearing a dancing dress with cherries on it. The bottom of it swung saucily as she moved to avoid the stampede of racing man-horses.

"Why don't they just stand up on two legs and piggyback the riders to victory?" Chase asked, flattening himself against the wall.

"They're ponies, not satyrs."

"I couldn't tell by the tail. Is that inserted in their . . ."

"Ass," she finished. "Yup."

"Well." Chase took a large drink. He seemed to be doing that a lot here. "That's something you don't see every day."

"Actually, it is," Anya told him.

Back in Vegas all those years ago he and Colleen had

double-dated with Anya and her boyfriend, but he didn't remember much about hanging out with Anya. Even back then, he'd been obsessed with Colleen. But from what he could recall, Anya didn't take any shit and was a lot of fun.

"So you're a model, too? Got any tips for a beginner?" he asked.

"Take every job you can. No matter how small or weird. Get your name out there. Of course, you already have a name, so it might be a little easier on you."

Chase was comfortable talking about fashion and Couture. It was safer, and he didn't feel like such a rube. "The runway wasn't what I was expecting. The lights are really hot, and the flashbulbs nearly blinded me."

"That was nothing," she said, snorting. "At least you didn't have the designer screaming at you during outfit changes that you're ruining his career."

"That sounds like fun." Chase probably would have told the guy off. At least Max didn't have a big ego and a chip on his shoulder.

"It's not always like that. I really dig getting the makeup and hair done. I feel like a human Barbie doll, but in a good way." Anya frowned. "It's all about the clothes anyway. You appeared to be having a blast up there."

"I was a little nervous," he said. "But then I saw Colleen and it centered me. You don't know where she is, do you?" People were starting to pair off—in some cases in threes and fours. Yowza. He had nights like that. They were few and far between, but he guessed that was the status quo down here.

"Yup."

Chase waited, but Anya seemed content to eat the cherry out of her drink and watch Clint filming the pony race. The riders were on their second lap. Chase wondered if anyone was taking bets, because he had his money on one chick who was beating the hell out of her horse. After a few more moments of silence, Chase forced himself to sound casual and polite. "Where is she?"

"She's in her dungeon with Dante." Anya didn't even glance back at him. Which was a good thing, because the news hit him in the face like one of Colleen's slaps.

"What?" So much for polite.

Anya took a step away.

"Sorry. Which room is that?" He looked around the club. It could be anywhere. He hadn't exactly been paying attention to his surroundings last time. He was going to tie that smarmy bastard's dick in a knot.

"You'll never find it. She left orders not to be disturbed."

"What are they doing in the dungeon?"

"They're not fucking," Anya said.

His blood pressure ratcheted down a notch. "How do you know?"

"Well, unless Dante agreed to switch, it's not going to happen. Although I'd love to be a fly on the wall if he did." Anya whistled. "Dante's a pretty hard-core Dom. But Colleen is the prima Domme-a."

Chase wasn't sure he even wanted to know what all that meant, so he got to the important part. "What *are* they doing, then?"

"Last time she whipped him with a bullwhip." She blinked up innocently at him.

"What?" It came out a little less sharper this time, but louder than he wanted.

"But I think Dante thought that was too sub of him to continue. So I think she's negotiating with him to borrow one of his slaves."

"She wants to whip one of his slaves?" Chase wasn't sure how he felt about that. Aside from Better him than me.

"I try not to get into any of the details. But if she merely wanted someone to whip, she'd just find a pain sub for the evening. No, if she's interviewing for a slave, then it's mostly for sex."

"What?" There went his blood pressure again. He could feel the vein in his head pounding.

"Yeah, her last sex slave wanted another Mistress, so Colleen let him go. After all the trouble of training him. She lost a damned fine accountant, too."

"She was fucking her accountant?" Absently Chase wondered what they symptoms of a stroke were, because he was sweating and light-headed, and there was a pain in his chest.

Anya shrugged. "If he pleased her. Mostly he lived to serve."

"I don't even know what that means." Chase needed to talk to Colleen about this.

Anya's hand on his arm shocked him. He wasn't expecting a friendly touch. It seemed everyone here was hostile or indifferent to him.

"The key is, Chase, do you want to understand it? Because you're not going to get Colleen without it. You're too vanilla and she's too rocky road, if you get my meaning."

"Why are you telling me this? Colleen and I always end up detonating. I figured since you were her friend, you'd hate me."

"I did hate you. I was there to pick up the pieces when you couldn't keep your dick in your pants."

"My dick . . . ," Chase started off saying, and then realized how ridiculous the conversation could get. "That whole situation was a big misunderstanding that took us ten years to sort out. We're on a different path now."

Anya sighed. "I can see that. Listen, Colleen needs someone to love her. And not in the she-needs-a-man-to-be-complete way. I mean she should have someone cherish her again, like Alfie did."

Chase flinched, and Anya's grip tightened.

"I knew Alfie. He loved her. He gave her confidence. He was just what she needed at that time. And let's face it"— Anya let him go—"he was rich and powerful, and he protected her."

"I could have—"

"But you didn't," Anya spat out, drilling him in the chest with her finger. "Colleen isn't like your little girlfriends. She's a fucking force of nature. If you get in bed with the tornado, things are going to get shaken up, to say the least. I want to know, are you in it for the long haul? Because if you want a hit and run . . ." Anya spread her arms to take in the entire club. "Then take your pick."

"I want her," he said.

Anya smirked. "Good. Then you're going to have to be a sex slave."

A few hours later, Chase was making his way up to Shira's, where he knew Colleen was meeting with the reporter for some French magazine. He'd promised the guy an interview if he spilled the beans about what Colleen said to him. Armed with Anya's information, some of which Chase wished he could bleach out of his brain—other parts sounded damned interesting—he and Colleen were going to negotiate some hard limits.

Colleen's conversation with him at the Hot Spot suddenly made more sense. Hard limits: Exclusivity—check. No pain —check. Soft limits: Having sex in public. Not a problem as long as they were discreet. Chase had this. Now all he had to do was convince Colleen to give him another chance.

She spotted him as soon as he entered the restaurant. Her glance shifted to the nearest exits.

Oh no you don't.

Chase slid into the booth next to her, effectively trapping her in. "How about that interview?" he said to the reporter.

Colleen looked like she wanted to dump her iced tea in his lap, so he put his hand on her thigh. She started, but aside from that didn't move away from his touch.

"Excellent, Monsieur Fairwood. I'm so glad you could join us," the reporter said.

"Thrilled," Colleen said, shooting him a death glare.

But he noticed she didn't shove his hand away. So he moved it up under her skirt and traced circles on her inner thigh. She nearly choked on her drink, but instead of throwing it in his face, bless her, she shifted and spread her legs.

Chase completely missed what the reporter asked him. "I'm sorry, could you repeat that?"

"Do you have any designing plans of your own?"

Giving a chuckle, Chase shook his head. "Hell no. I'll leave the creating to the people who have talent. Like Max and Colleen here."

When the reporter shifted his gaze to Colleen, Chase pushed his hand a little higher. Her skin was soft and creamy. He could touch her for hours. A slight tremor went through her, and he was hard pressed to hide his grin. She still wanted him.

Luckily, the reporter was more captivated by Colleen's face to notice that Chase's body language was off. Colleen leaned forward to laugh at something the reporter said. Her body shifted closer to the table, effectively keeping the reporter in the dark. It also brought his fingertips in contact with her silk panties.

He circled his fingers around until he felt wetness. Her thighs quivered against his fingers, but she wasn't paying any attention to him. She had the best game face he'd ever seen. Colleen was enchanting the reporter with her bedroom eyes and her seductive smiles. If he hadn't had hand between her legs, Chase might have gotten jealous. As it was, he wanted to do so much more.

"So how did you two first meet?" the reporter asked.

Colleen tensed, so he flicked his fingers faster over the wet silk.

"I met her at one of the casinos," Chase said. He wasn't going to mention that she had been a stripper or anything like that. "She was assigned to me. I think her job was to make me spend all my money."

"I made things easier for Chase to stay at the table." Colleen shrugged. "He was pretty easy. He liked Scotch and chocolate chip cookies."

"Not at the same time," Chase cut in, pinching her thigh in retaliation.

"We grew apart, our lives taking off in different directions," she continued.

"And now fate has brought us back together." Chase found the edge of her panties and eased a finger in. God, she was molten heat. He couldn't reach any further without it being obvious he was finger-fucking her, so he eased back to small little circles on that sopping wet silk. Those panties were going to be in his teeth tonight if it was the last thing he did.

"Professionally," Colleen butted in, shoving his shoulder playfully for their audience. He got the message and removed his hand.

Colleen's phone rang, and she dug through her purse to grab it. "Yes? . . . All right. I'll be right there." She turned to the reporter. "Didier, I'm so sorry, but I have to cut this short. I'm sure Monsieur Fairwood can finish off the interview." She pushed him, and Chase didn't have a choice but to let her out of the booth.

"One moment, Didier," Chase said, and escorted Colleen toward the door of the restaurant. When they were far enough away from the table so the reporter didn't have a chance of overhearing, he said, "I need to see you later."

"No, you *want* to see me later. That's not going to happen." She pasted a bright smile on her face, but her tone could have poisoned a rattlesnake.

"I'm sorry." Chase looked down at his feet. "I was wrong. I'll do anything to make it up to you." He glanced up, hoping his sincerity was written all over his face.

"Too little too late. Now let go of me before I cause a scene." Colleen jiggled her arm out of his grasp.

It was time to play his trump card. "Can you give me a sense of how hard you hit with a crop?"

"Don't tempt me, Chase," she said, but stopped when she registered that his tone was serious and interested. "Why do you ask?" she whispered.

"Are you a sadist?"

She blinked. "I have tendencies. But no, I don't classify myself as a sadist. Again, why are you asking this?"

He had her on the run. Now she knew how flabbergasted he had been the other night when she threw all this stuff at him.

"I want to talk about hard limits."

"Why?" She flicked a glance over his shoulder at the reporter.

"Because I want to be your only sex slave."

Chase wished he had a camera to capture the expression on her face. This might be the only time she had ever been speechless. Then her eyes narrowed and she swept him a look from top to bottom. He resisted the urge to squirm.

"You don't have the slightest idea what it means to serve or offer up submission."

"Teach me. You're the instructor."

He had her. He knew it by the set of her jaw that she was considering his offer.

"Listen carefully, Chase. Because this is your last fucking chance with me."

Hope burst through him. He was in. He could kiss Anya for giving him the words to do this.

"You finish up with Didier over there. You make it sound like I'm a genius and Max's line is the next big thing. Then you're going to come up to my office and we're going to hash this out."

"Negotiate our hard and soft limits." Chase grinned. He was getting the hang of it.

"There will be no negotiation. I'll take your hard limits into account. But you, as a slave, don't get an opinion. The trust you give to me as a dominant is that you tell me what your hard limits are and then you trust me, no matter how close I push to that limit. You trust that I'm a professional and that I am seeking the same pleasure as you. Now, do you really understand the relationship you're trying to get into?"

"Yes," he lied.

"Then you're going to try out."

"Try out?" Anya hadn't mentioned anything like this. Chase didn't like the idea that he might have competition.

"To put it in football terms, I just selected you from the draft. You've got the rest of the night as your preseason. If you make the cut, you'll be my sex slave. If you don't, you only come here for Max, and you don't ever touch me again. Do we have a deal?"

Chase hesitated. He didn't like thinking about not touching her again.

"I'll treat you as I would anyone new to the lifestyle," she continued. "But if you think your actions in the dungeons will be any different from any other slave's, you need to walk away right now."

"Will we have sex?" he asked.

"On my terms," she said.

"I'm your man." Chase winked.

"We'll see about that. I'll be in my office waiting for you."

"Why not in the dungeon?" he asked.

"You have to earn your way back into my dungeon." Colleen perused him again, and he felt the heat in her gaze like it was her tongue taking in every inch of him. "Don't keep me waiting too long."

He watched the confident sway of her hips and wondered just what the hell Anya had gotten him into.

CHAPTER 8

"Well, love me tender and call me Elvis." Colleen waited until she was behind closed doors before sinking against it. Chase Fairwood was going to attempt submission. It would never work. She was crazy to take him on as a slave. He was used to being the one calling the shots. Hell, his modus operandi was to burn hot, go off like TNT, sulk, and then wonder why she was still pissed at him. He was a grenade, and she had given up on throwing herself on those types of people a long time ago. Yet he wanted her. Maybe enough to let her take him to new heights. She was actually shaking with anticipation.

This could be a turning point for her. With Max's new line and Chase helping out, it finally seemed as if she'd get some good press from a Paris magazine. And that might trickle down to better coverage in the States. She'd like to get rid of the "gold-digging whore" mantle that she had been forced to wear ever since marrying Alfie. Finally she could be recognized for her abilities. Her public face would be as the head of Couture, the "it" place to be for fashion, and her private face could be the head dominatrix of Club Inferno with a worthy lover at her side. She wanted that so badly it burned into her soul and took her breath.

Unlocking the door to her office so that Chase could get in, Colleen checked her schedule to make sure she had nothing else planned for the night. Nefertiti was long off work, and Colleen hoped she was letting Istvahn pamper her. Her schedule, it turned out, was free. Now, to decide how to handle this.

Should she get into her dungeon gear or let Chase strip her? Walking over to her floor-to-ceiling window, she gazed up into the night sky. No. This had to be handled as if he was a stranger coming to the dungeon for the first time. If she didn't want to scare the crap out of Chase again, Colleen had to go slow.

Although Chase sure hadn't been thinking slow when he tried to finger her at the restaurant. It had taken all she had not to let him go further. Definitely not what she wanted Didier to report on, that was damned sure. Still, the fact that Chase felt comfortable playing with her again in public gave her some hope.

It surprised her how much she wanted this second chance. Before the dungeon fiasco, Colleen had just wanted to fuck him and get it out of her system. But . . . it had hurt to see him walk away. She wasn't going to investigate her feelings too closely. Not when it could all blow up in her face.

Kicking off her shoes, Colleen pulled out the couch by the window so it lay flat like a bed. With Chase's bad knees, he couldn't kneel, so they would probably be horizontal while they worked out a few things. She made the bed with thick cotton sheets, the thread count so high they were almost flannel, but they were softer than cashmere. Turning on the sound system, she put on some soft jazz, then dialed on the fake fireplace.

Admiring her work, Colleen thought it hit the right

amount of cozy. Then she activated a screen to block off that section, so that her office appeared professional, if a bit dull without the erotic art visible on the far wall.

She was pretending to play solitaire on her computer when Chase walked in.

"Close the door and lock it," she said without glancing up. Her pulse sped, but she forced herself to remain aloof.

"May I sit?" he asked.

She couldn't help the small lift of her lips at how hard he was trying to be deferential. Nodding, Colleen powered down her computer to give him her full attention. He sat across from her, staring intensely.

Looking into his handsome face, all her plans flew out of her head. She was going to take whatever he was willing to give—if he didn't fuck up this part. "So tell me again why you ran out of my dungeon like Michael Vick at an ASPCA meeting, and then two weeks later you're ready to be my submissive."

Chase cleared his throat. "I was an idiot."

Colleen gestured that he should go on.

"I wasn't expecting the dungeon and the club under Couture. I figured we were going back to your room."

"I did come on a little strong," she admitted. "I'm sorry if I frightened you."

"I was more freaked out than anything else." He ran his hand over his face. "I should have turned around and begged forgiveness then."

"Are you still freaked out?" Colleen got up from around her desk and stood behind his chair.

"No." He tracked her motion, but when she laid her hands on his shoulders, he stared straight ahead.

"Tell me exactly what you're looking for." Colleen lifted his shirt over his head and tossed it on the floor.

She caressed the hard muscles on his shoulders and arms.

Ten years hadn't changed his body all that much. Dragging her nails lightly down his back, she smiled at his contented groan. Colleen still remembered everything he liked, every button to push to get him to go wild. She wondered if he remembered her the same way.

"This is nice," he whispered. "I want to be your lover."

"Anything else?" Colleen ran her hands over his chest, leaning forward to lick his ear.

"I want to please you."

"Good," she purred in his ear. "I like that. What else?"

"I want . . ." He sucked in a sharp breath when her teeth found his neck. "I want to experience this submission and dominance with you. With only you."

Colleen's heart was hammering. This was what Dante should have said but didn't. This was the right reason to work with a Domme.

"Okay," she said, pulling herself together. "Now, what don't you want?"

"I don't want to share you," he ground out.

There was the exclusivity that she had wanted from Jake. "Agreed. We won't have sex with anyone else. But . . ."

He tensed under her hands.

"You need to realize the difference between sex and sexual instruction. I will still work with my clients." Before he could interject, Colleen added. "But you will be with me during these sessions as your schedule permits. And hopefully you will see that what I do is very satisfying and necessary, but it's not cheating on you." She yanked his head back so she could stare into his eyes.

He smiled lazily and settled back against her.

"What else don't you want?" She flicked her tongue over his earlobe.

Chase swallowed. "I don't want to do fire, electricity, scat or water sports, or knife play."

Someone had been reading up during the past two weeks. Colleen bit back a laugh. She must have really given him something to think about. "Those are definitely things most beginners avoid. I've never started out with any of those. I generally don't create scenes with them, either. If you were interested in those activities, I would have to refer you to another Mistress."

"Good," he said. "No humiliation or pain."

Colleen felt it was time to give him a little reality check. "What about this?" She pinched his nipple and he groaned.

"That would be all right."

She nipped his ear.

"Yeah . . . oh God, do that again."

Colleen did and then breathed in his ear. "Seems to me a little pain is okay. So let's make that a soft limit."

He nodded.

"You say, 'Yes, Mistress.'"

"Yes, Mistress," Chase said, with a trace of humor in his voice.

"No humiliation," she agreed. Chase wasn't the type to crawl around on all fours while she verbally abused him. And they still had some baggage that she wouldn't want to come out during play if they hadn't resolved it. "You will wear a mask when we're in public together as a Domme and submissive. That way no one will recognize you."

"They'd have to be idiots not to figure out who it is," Chase blustered.

"The people who know you and me, yes. Strangers will have no idea. It will free up your inhibitions."

"Okay," he said. "I mean, yes, Mistress."

He was a quicker study than fricking Dante, that was for damn sure.

"Outside of the dungeon," Chase said, turning his head to look at her, "I don't want to play games. I want you to be

Colleen and me to be Chase. I'm not going to do housework naked."

Colleen's lips twitched. "Pity. But fortunately, I already have a cleaning staff. And it's tiring to Domme 24/7. I'm on board with all of that. You only call me Mistress when we're playing and I'll only expect your submission when we're having sex. I know this whole thing isn't your kink. I get that. I'm going to have a great time introducing you to the life-style. We'll go slow at first. No more storming away. We stay and talk things out."

Like we should have ten years ago.

"I'll try and keep my temper in check. I know I can react first and regret it later," Chase said with a nod. "Aside from all of that, I'm all yours. Now, what do *you* want?"

Clever boy. Not many people asked that question. "I want your trust. Your absolute submission. I want to have earth-shattering orgasms with you."

Chase swallowed audibly. "Yeah."

"I demand fidelity." She tugged his hair in warning. "And you need to communicate with me. I need to know if what I'm doing is good for you. If you fake it or endure it because you're thinking to please me, you won't."

"What about the long term? Are we a couple now, officially?"

"Let's get through the week without killing each other first, hmmm?" Colleen chuckled in his ear, going back to nibbling on it.

"I could come just from that," he sighed, reaching back to stroke her hair.

"That reminds me," Colleen said, coming up for air. "You have to ask my permission to come, and if I say no, you don't do it. Understand?"

Chase shifted uncomfortably. "I suppose I have to trust you not to give me blue balls?"

"You're not fourteen, Chase, and I'm not going to keep you going for four hours. Teasing you isn't a trip to Tiffany's, for Pete's sake."

He sniggered.

"I'm going to train you to hold in your orgasm until the best possible moment. Being denied the need to come makes the next time, when you actually do, worth every agonizing moment."

"If you say so," Chase mused.

"If you please me, I'll please you. Right now, you please me." Colleen moved around to his front and straddled him on the chair.

"Do I have to ask if I can touch you?" Chase's hands twitched.

"Yes."

"May I touch you?" His voice was hoarse.

She nodded, leaning in to give him an openmouthed kiss that was all tongue and sweetness. The fever that spiked every time their mouths touched hit like a tidal wave. Chase wrapped his arms tight around her. Colleen held on to his shoulders, digging her nails in slightly and let herself go. They kissed until they were breathless and Colleen's lips were puffy. Her clothes were askew from Chase's manhandling her while their mouths made love. Chase's cock strained against her panties, and it took all her effort to climb off him. She slapped at his hands when they tried to drag her back. Colleen pointed at him in warning. He held his hands up in surrender.

"Do you like pleasing me?" she asked, stepping out of her skirt.

"I want to throw you on that desk and fuck you," Chase growled.

Colleen considered it as she unbuttoned her blouse. "Take your pants off, slave. I want to see you naked."

"Yes, Mistress," Chase said eagerly, and shed his clothes.

She could bend over the desk and Chase would be inside her before her chest hit her blotter. Anticipation coiled through her. It would be fast and furious and over far too soon. No. As much as she wanted him inside her, she wanted him to fuck her for a long time.

So Colleen deliberately left on her underwear. But her mouth was still dry, and her breasts felt heavy and ached for attention. Her clit was so swollen, the slightest friction would send her over the edge. Grabbing Chase by the cock, she pulled him forward. Hitting the control on the room's partition, Colleen stepped behind the curtain and led him to the couch she had prepared.

"Nice," Chase said. "Honey, I need to touch you."

"Patience," she chided, reluctantly letting him go so she could position herself on the bed. She lay back against the window, the cool glass hardening her nipples more. Spreading her legs, Colleen motioned Chase on the bed. "Sit on the edge. How's your knee?"

"It's fine. More than fine. Can I come up there by you?"

"Not just yet."

She watched him clench his fists and wondered if this small thing would be the end of it all. If she were smart, she'd haul him up her and fuck him before he stormed out again. Colleen traced her nipple through her bra. Chase's attention riveted on her fingers. That was better.

"Have you picked out a safe word?"

"Broccoli," he said.

She wasn't sure if he was serious or not, but it worked as well as any other word. "If your knee starts to ache, use it. I don't think I'll give you cause to safeword for a while yet. When I start pushing those limits of yours, you'll need to tell me when to back off."

Chase cleared his throat. "I will."

"We need to talk about punishment," she said, sliding her hand into her panties. She played with her clit while he watched. "You're being such a good slave right now, but I know you, Chase. You'll step over the line. And when you do, I'll need to punish you. Right now, I want to fuck you just as much as you want me."

"Thank you, God," he muttered under his breath.

"And since this is your first night, I'm going to take it easy on you—as long as you follow directions." Colleen moved her finger faster.

"I'll do anything you want me to do. Just please, let me do it."

"I want you to watch me come," she said. "If you think of a punishment that I can dole out to you by the time I come, I'll allow you to rip off my panties and lick me until I come again. If you don't, I'm going to send you home and we can try again tomorrow. Got it?"

"I'm going to get it," he said.

"Better hurry." Colleen bit her lip and rubbed faster.

Her eyes were half closed and her mouth had opened to sigh her pleasure when he blurted out, "You can spank me."

What happened to that being a hard limit?

Colleen was still reeling from that when he lunged across the bed. Pressing kisses on her belly, Chase pushed her panties to the side and thrust two fingers into her. All thoughts fled as Colleen's head knocked back against the window. Chase grunted and pulled her down toward him, so her head bounced on the couch.

"Chase," she gasped out as he shimmied her underwear down her legs.

"I can't rip wet silk, Mistress. Allow me to make it up to you." And then he was between her legs, lapping at her eagerly.

Colleen spread out on the bed, tilting her head back to see

the night sky. Stars were exploding up there, or maybe it was all happening behind her eyelids. "Chase," she encouraged, pumping her hips against his mouth.

Chase's groans turned her on. His arms were wrapped around her waist, his face buried against her slick wetness. Tonguing her swollen clit, he was enthusiastic and nearly incoherent in his interjections.

"God. Baby. So good. Want you. So much. Fuck. So damn wet."

She rode his mouth into another orgasm.

He was suddenly up by her breasts. "Do I have to ask permission to fuck you? Because damn, baby. Please. Let me fuck you."

Head whirling, Colleen tried for some control. As much as she wanted it, she had to go slow with him, so not tonight. But that didn't mean they couldn't have a good time. "Get on your back," she ordered.

He flipped over eagerly. "Climb on me. I want to feel that wet pussy on my cock."

She didn't have the heart to chastise him for giving orders. But she could make him wait for it. Kneeling up on the bed, she unfastened her bra. Her breasts bounced free and she sucked in a long breath.

"Colleen," he moaned.

She straddled his legs down low by his knees and leaned over to take his cock between her breasts.

Chase bucked and swore as her nipples dragged across his abdomen. Sandwiched between her breasts, his penis rubbed her chest. Liking the sensation of sliding him between them, Colleen dipped her chin to lick at the head.

"I am going to go off right now," he warned.

Colleen immediately stopped and lay down next to him. "No, you aren't." She told him. "Your orgasms belong to me, remember. You have to ask for my permission to come."

"Don't tease me, baby. It's been too long. I need to be inside you."

Colleen tossed a leg over his stomach. His cock pressed into her thigh. "You will," she promised. "But you're right. It has been too long. Too long to rush this. But I am going to have mercy on you. Just this once."

She kissed him again, but before he could deepen the kiss, Colleen pulled away. "Play with my breasts. Suck on them while you stroke yourself. You're going to come all over your stomach first."

Chase wasted no time capturing the nipple she brushed over his lips. Colleen cried out at the hard tug. Yes. This. Exactly. She watched him pump his cock, mesmerized by his fast hard jerks. His lips tightened around her nipple as ropy spurts of come hit his chest.

"Oh," he shuddered, still lavishing her breasts with his tongue and teeth.

"Lie still." Colleen gently pushed him back on the couch and got up to go to the bathroom for some towels. She cleaned him up with a warm soapy washcloth and a thick fluffy towel. Then she cuddled up next to him and stroked his hair while they watched the electric fireplace.

His jaw cracked when he yawned. "I will not fall asleep," he said, turning his head to capture the soft kisses she was peppering along his jaw.

"It's all right if you do."

"Damn it, I'm not going to spend our first night snoring on a couch while a beautiful woman lies on top of me."

Colleen nuzzled his neck, seeing his eyelids go heavy. "You have my permission to rest. You're going to need it tomorrow. I've got double sessions booked. I'm going to need my sub. Not to mention that you have to be out of here before Nefertiti gets in or I'll never hear the end of it."

He hugged her to him. She cast her leg over his, and they fit back together as if they'd never been apart.

"Just a quick nap," he said, sleep coating his voice. "Then it's round two." He sighed. "This feels right. You here with me. Want you." Chase's voice trailed off into a soft snore.

Colleen thought about going down on him until he was hard and then riding him until they both came again. But he was right. This was nice. Her eyelids fluttered, too. Some Domme she was. She was going soft. Colleen cuddled closer in his arms and listened to his breathing. It had been a long few weeks. Tomorrow they could pick up where they'd left off.

CHAPTER 9

Chase was pretty sure that when his sister called him tonight and asked him how his weekend had gone, he was going to just say "Good" and leave it at that. Because it was a lot easier than saying he'd had a successful fashion show, seen men being ridden like ponies with tail appendages shoved in their asses, gotten back together with his old girlfriend, and watched a married couple have prison sex.

All the while dressed like a reject from an S&M porn flick.

He had slept through the night like a rock and woken up to the erotic movements of Colleen's tongue on his cock. After a blow job that made him forget his name, she kicked him out and told him he had an hour to grab a shower and some coffee before he had to report to the dungeon for their morning session.

His outfit had been a little over the top. The black leather ski mask attached in the back with Velcro straps. Chase was shirtless, but he had on black silk pants that were loose enough to hide his growing hard-on.

When he came into the dungeon, Colleen had been fluffing up pillows like a Martha Stewart dominatrix. Her black pants looked painted on. She wore a tight-fitting corset that pushed her ample breasts together. Chase wanted to lick every inch of her.

She had grabbed his cock through the pants and pumped it. Her silk-wrapped fist nearly had him coming again. Chase couldn't get enough of her. He was a lucky man to have Colleen's undivided attention. She brought him to the brink of orgasm and then sat him in a wide, plush chair.

"This is where you'll observe the session," she said. "If you please me, you'll be rewarded. If not . . ." Colleen smacked her gloved hands together.

The morning session started out all right. A cute couple wanted to play around with handcuffs and flavored lotion. He spent most of the time staring at Colleen, which was a pleasure all in of itself. She was gorgeous and she was all his, even if she did monitor the action on the bed a little too closely for his liking. But true to her word, she kept her clothes on and no one touched her. She only touched the couple to readjust a position.

The couple hadn't done anything more than get naked and kiss and grope. But they left the dungeon so hot for each other, Chase would have bet cash money that they were humping in the parking lot before going home.

Afterward, Colleen had been called away on a phone call, so after changing into his normal clothes, he had lunch with Clint and Max in the Irish bar over on the Couture side. They'd talked about the catalog shoot they were going to do tomorrow. Chase was a little nervous, but they said they were going to bring in a few more experienced models for diversity. So maybe he could watch the models and pretend he knew what he was doing; maybe one of them would take pity on him and show him the ropes. How hard could it be? Just dress up and smile for the camera.

Before he could ask any detailed questions, though, Chase had been summoned back into Club Inferno. When he got there, Colleen had transformed the dungeon from an IKEA bedroom display to a prison cell, complete with leaky toilet.

"You missed your calling," he had joked. "You should have been an interior decorator. I love what you've done with the place."

"Did you have fun this morning?" She'd come into his arms for a nice, lingering kiss.

"And last night." He had smoothed his hand down her body and held her against him. Chase cupped her amazing ass. "When can I fuck you?"

"Soon," Colleen promised. "This afternoon I'm going to test your comfort zone in the next session. This next couple likes to role-play."

"Like the locker room scene you did for me," Chase had said, and then winced. Shit. The last thing he wanted to do was bring up that fiasco. But Colleen had merely been amused.

"Not exactly," she had said. "You're an observer only again. So sit back in your chair and enjoy the view."

He really appreciated that she didn't make him kneel like the other subs. When he asked her about it she told him it was her responsibility to make sure he didn't get injured, and prolonged kneeling would aggravate his injury. Pride warred with common sense, but in the end Colleen wouldn't have it any other way. So he got to sit in a comfy chair and watch people have sex. Not a bad gig when you came down to it.

It had been pretty hot to watch the afternoon couple prep for the role play. It was like watching a live sex show. He had gone to one in Amsterdam, but it didn't really do it for him one way or the other. It was just live porn. He liked a more mutual activity. The jury was still out if this qualified, since his girlfriend was the instructor and not a participant. In any case, he was far from bored.

"Be careful when using a foreign object. There isn't a stopgap, like there is with the vagina. You don't want to end up in the emergency room."

Chase winced, but cleared his face of emotion when Colleen narrowed a glare at him. How could she even see his expression under this thing? His nose itched. But he had been given orders to remain perfectly still, and he wasn't about to risk a spanking no matter how much the leather mask bugged the shit out of him.

He was still trying to figure this kink thing out. Colleen didn't seem to be aroused. He'd seen enough of that last night and in the past to know when she was turned on and revving hot. But she did look different. Content? Centered. She was good at what she was doing, if the moans of the couple on the bed were any indication.

The prison scene wasn't doing much for him. So he let his mind wander back to Vegas, when he and Colleen used the city like their personal playground. A smile flitted across his face as he remembered the time they'd gotten so drunk that they decided to go on the roller coasters and flash the cameras. He'd been fined ten thousand dollars and had almost been benched when the pictures made the rounds on AOL. It was totally worth it. So maybe he was a little kinky.

"Grab the bars of the cage, like this." Colleen came up along side of the couple and demonstrated.

Chase's body reacted as if he were the one positioned behind her. It happened quickly and without warning. As if she felt the change, Colleen glanced up at him. Her hair was back in a complicated braid, away from her face, so he could see into those wide blue eyes. Her hands were in silk gloves, wrapped around the bars of the fake jail cell. The corset she was wearing strained tighter as she bent over and her lush, full breasts threatened to spill out. Wiggling her hips, she play-acted getting rammed from behind. Making sure he was watching, she pantomimed moaning.

Yeah, that.

He swallowed past his dry throat. She needed to be out of those clothes. The dungeon was a nuisance. Chase wanted her alone and needing him, and he wished she was on the bed on her hands and knees.

"Good," Colleen said to the couple as she winked at him. Straightening up, she bent toward the woman who had clutched the bars like Colleen asked her. "Are you doing all right?"

The woman nodded. "I like it when he goes slow like this."

The man clutched her shoulder as he held himself in place. "I'm ready to come," he panted.

"Use the vibrator on her clit. She'll move her hips and that's how you'll finish."

He nodded, turning on the little wand. The woman cried out and, true to Colleen's word, wiggled her hips for more. As the couple worked on climaxing, Colleen came out of the fake jail cell and walked over to him.

"Are you hard?" she whispered in his ear.

The grunting and moaning in the jail cell was adding to his desire. "Yes, Ma'am," he said.

She sat on his lap, facing outward. Rubbing herself on him, Colleen eased back so they could both watch the couple. The man finished with an incoherent roar, staying inside the woman and working the vibrator until she shrieked her orgasm out. Colleen clapped her gloved hands.

"Very nice! I want ten minutes of cuddling and then take a shower together. Come back once you're dried off and we'll switch positions."

"What does that mean?" Chase whispered in her ear,

hoping she didn't think they were going to go at it in the cell while the couple watched.

Instead of answering, Colleen slid off his lap and walked toward an armoire in the corner. He missed her warmth on him and shifted uncomfortably. She came back with an alarming contraption. Chase remembered at the last minute not to balk. He just sat there as she approached.

"She's going to wear a strap-on," Colleen said, and tossed it on the table next to him. "Do you have a problem with that?"

"Is she going to use it on me?"

Colleen frowned. "Do you want her to?"

"No." *Is she out of her mind?*

"Did you tell me that you wanted to be exclusive in your playing?"

"Yes." Chase could see where this was going. He was going to get a spanking, he just knew it. And while the thought didn't please him, it didn't make him want to run for the hills, either. Maybe if he was lucky, they could turn it into some hot and heavy sex afterward. He needed to be inside her so badly, he was willing to do just about anything.

"Then this is the last warning you're going to get," Colleen said. "You may ask questions when it concerns you. I told you when we entered into this scene what your role was. You are not a participant. You're here to learn. Are you learning?"

"Yes, Ma'am," he said.

"You've displeased me." Colleen had a small smile, and a cute dimple was showing in her cheek. He wanted to stick his tongue in the divot. "How are you going to make it up to me?"

Chase had a few ideas, starting with fucking her hard against the wall until she left bloody half moons on his shoulders. But at the last minute he remembered himself. "By doing whatever you want."

"Excellent." Her smile alone was worth the anticipated pain. "You're taking me out for pizza after this."

Colleen almost laughed at Chase's expression. Not what he had been expecting, that's for sure. The rest of the session went as well as the first half. Madison excelled in getting her husband relaxed for the role play by "forcing" him to lube up her strap-on dildo while she went down on him. Madison needed a little help with the logistics of the equipment, but then went at it enthusiastically. Unlike his wife, Rick liked it hard and fast and jerked himself off while she pumped away at him from behind.

Colleen pretended not to see Chase flinch and squirm. Hard limit, maybe. She stood behind Madison to make sure her angle was all right. Chase's eyes were glazing over, so Colleen decided to wake him up a bit. Stepping back from the couple on the bed, she unhooked the first two fastenings on her corset, which freed her breasts. She had Chase's full attention as she offered them to him. Unlike during most of her sessions, Colleen was pleasantly aroused. She liked introducing Chase to his first dungeon experiences. Rolling her nipples between her silk-clad fingers, Colleen wished Chase liked more public displays. She knew her couple wouldn't mind it if Chase pleasured her while they watched.

Fuck me? she mouthed at him.

He gave a short nod. *Let's go,* he mouthed back.

Colleen shifted and stuffed the girls back into her top, fastening up the hooks.

Rick's body spasmed as he came in thick jerks across the cot.

"Pull out," Colleen ordered Madison, who obeyed her without question. "Roll over," she told Rick. Madison unbuckled the belt, tossing the contraption on the floor. "Sit on his face. Don't get up until you come."

Madison moved eagerly on top of her husband.

"I'll see you next week." Colleen said to them. Crooking her finger at Chase, she strode out of the dungeon.

They made it to the room next door, where their street clothes were, before they were kissing. Grabbing him by the shoulders, she pinned him against the closed door. Colleen wished she was wearing a skirt so she could just climb on top of Chase and ride him. As it was, he was having a hard time peeling her pants down. That was the one thing about tight, hot dungeon wear—it took forever to get out of. The next time they were in a private scene, she was going to wear a nice rippable dress. The thought of Chase literally tearing her clothes off made her desperate. She fumbled his jeans open and gripped his cock.

Chase inhaled and pulled back from their heated kiss to work on her corset. Stroking him while he figured out the hooks and clasps on her corset, Colleen watched his fingers shake.

"Help me," he muttered.

Letting him go, with regret, she sat on a long and wide bench. "Take off my boots."

There wasn't any time for finesse. But she admired him on his knees in front of her. Ripping the zippers down, he tossed the boots aside. Then he was tugging off the tight leather pants as she unlaced the corset. Her breasts spilled free over the top of it.

"Leave it on," he said, laying her back on the wide bench. "Please. Ma'am. Fuck. Am I doing this right?" Pants half off, he covered her body, slipping inside her.

Bliss.

She had already been wet and ready for him. He sank in deep and paused.

"Wow," he puffed.

Wow was right. Colleen wanted this moment to last

forever, them joined together, trembling on the edge of something fantastic.

"You're doing just fine," she assured him, capturing him by tightening her legs around his waist, securing him close. He wouldn't be walking out on her now.

Chase pressed closer and cupped her breasts in his hands. "I want you so much, I can't make this last."

Nearly bent in two, Colleen grabbed on to his forearms for balance. "I don't want you to. Fuck me."

Chase pounded into her, hard and fast. She didn't have time for any more orders, just for the utter satisfaction of being filled with his thickness. She dug her nails into him and gritted her teeth in pleasure at his rough pounding. Her breasts swayed in a heavy rhythm. His eyes were locked on them. She was glad they had fallen asleep last night. The end result now was so much more satisfying after the sweet buildup of cuddling and then the dungeon scenes.

"Yes. Harder. Faster." Colleen craved more from him.

Chase obliged. Gripping her hips, he stood up, straddling the bench. Colleen's shoulder blades were the only thing touching the bench as he manipulated their bodies so that he was controlling the punishing pace.

This couldn't have happened with this intensity if they hadn't fallen asleep wrapped in each other's arms. Raw sex. Pure pleasure.

"Chase," she cried out as the orgasm crashed over her, too far gone to stop. She was flying away without an anchor to this world.

"Mistress. May I come?"

A second wave tingled through her. He had remembered, even through all this pent up sexual desire. "Yes," she breathed.

He thrust deep. She wiggled around him, clamping her muscles to give him the best friction. Chase scrunched up his eyes and held her tight as his body jolted in pleasure. For a few moments after, the only sound in the room was their harsh breathing.

Chase came back to himself, reeling a bit. "Was that all right? Did I hurt you?" He released her hips and she lowered her legs.

"That was perfect." Colleen stood up and wrapped her arms around him. "Just perfect."

CHAPTER 10

C olleen floated on a cloud of bliss in the passenger's seat of Chase's Mercedes Roadster. His hands were strong and sure on the leather-covered shifter, just like they had been on her hips. She could still feel the imprint of his fingers. Kicking off her shoes, she toed the luxurious car mats. She half considered lifting her skirt up so he could see she wasn't wearing underwear, but she figured she'd let him find that out all on his own. Leaning back against the head-rest, Colleen turned to watch him drive. His profile capti-vated her, as it always did. As it always had.

"How are you doing?" she asked. There hadn't been a lot of space for aftercare in the dressing room. They had put their street clothes on and walked hand in hand to his car.

"I'm fan-freaking-tastic," he said, his grin wide and goofy. "And so are you. I'm looking forward to bringing you back to my place tonight and having sex in a bed. Are you on board with that?"

Colleen should stay at Couture. She shouldn't want to see Chase's apartment so badly. But she did. "I think I can rearrange my schedule."

"So how do you think I'm doing?" His sideways glance at her was serious.

"So far so good," she said. "We haven't tested this in fire yet."

"I thought I mentioned that was a hard limit," he teased.

Colleen laughed. "You liked the hot wax."

"I remember that night," he said. "We can do that again."

"We will, but what I meant was we haven't had to deal with anything awful yet. That will be the test of us, you know."

Chase frowned. "You shouldn't be so pessimistic. Awful things don't have to be inevitable."

"We've got a few awful things on our agenda," she told him.

"Like what?"

Colleen shook her head. "Not yet. I don't want to fight. I feel too damn good. I want to eat pizza and drink sweet syrupy soda. Then I want to see your bachelor pad and go all 9½ Weeks on you."

"Do I get to be Mickey Rourke?" he asked, accelerating past a slow-moving truck on the highway.

"No."

"I can live with that," he said. "I suppose you want me to take you down to Wooster Street?"

"Not unless you want to wait in line around the block. Take the State Street exit. There's a less well-known pizzeria with just as good, if not better, pizza than the Wooster Street one."

"Sacrilege," Chase told her mildly, but got off at the exit.

They parked in a commuter lot across the street from the restaurant, and as Colleen had known they would, they walked right in and got a table.

"You still hate pepperoni?" he asked after the waitress took their Foxon Park soda orders, a New Haven pizzeria staple. Birch beer for Colleen, who loved the wintergreen taste. And Iron Brew for Chase—a cross between root beer, cola, and cream soda.

"And do you still have an aversion to mushrooms?"

They looked at each other and said, "Plain cheese?" at the same time.

Colleen glanced away while he laughed. It was too easy, slipping back into their roles as if time had never separated them. If she didn't watch out, he'd have her heart as well as her body. And damned if that traitorous organ wasn't okay with that.

Not until they settled his animosity toward Alfie and not until he fully accepted her lifestyle. If Chase could weather those "awfuls," then she'd start thinking in terms of permanent. Right now it was temporary. Thrilling and new.

After some more negotiation, they decided on a small mozzarella and a small meatball. Colleen was pretty sure Chase was going to eat the meatball one all by himself.

"Are you nervous about tomorrow's catalog shoot?" Colleen asked, watching him from under her lashes. It was ridiculous to feel shy around him. She was a professional Domme, for chrissakes. Yet the part of her that remembered him as her first love still saw him as the man who'd won her heart by playing the worst game of blackjack she'd ever seen in order to ensure that she would tutor him privately on how to play. To this day, though, the dumb-ass probably hit on a twelve when the dealer was showing a six.

Some people never learn.

She wasn't sure if she was talking about him or herself.

"Yeah, I'm a little nervous about it." Chase gave her a half grin and reached over to hold her hand.

"You'll be either bored to tears or so tired from smiling you'll forget what you were ever nervous about."

"Clint's going to do a video of it."

Colleen sipped her soda. "Keep your pants on."

"What's that supposed to mean?"

"It means," Colleen said, "Clint is in charge of filming Club Inferno's pay website. He's a good cameraman, but watch out for the kinky stuff."

"I kinda doubt he wants to see me let it all hang out." Chase lowered his voice. "I don't want to be on the website, either, even if I am wearing a mask."

"I'd make more money if you didn't wear the mask," Colleen teased.

"Excuse me, Mr. Fairwood?" Two young kids came up to the table. "Can we have your autograph?"

Chase smiled apologetically at Colleen and turned to the kids. "Sure can. You guys football fans?"

Colleen watched him talk with the kids, asking them questions about school and their hobbies. He stood up to take a picture with them, and shook their parents' hands. She saw recognition hit their parents when they saw her, and soon the kids were shuffled away. *Quelle surprise*—no one wanted her autograph. But then again, she wasn't famous for playing football.

"So much for inconspicuous." Colleen gave a small smile.

"What do you mean?"

She inclined her head at the parents of the two kids. The mother was texting something. "You and I are probably going to make the Internet before our pizza gets here."

"Well, let's give them something to write about." Chase grabbed her hand and pressed a kiss into her palm.

"You don't know what you're getting into," Colleen said, but curled her hand around his strong jaw.

"I don't care what people say about me. And neither do you." He released her as the waitress brought over two round trays of pizza. Chase served her a piece of the pie, the cheese long and stringy.

"Hot," he said, and stuck his fingers in his mouth.

"Don't burn the roof of your mouth," she warned.

Chase reluctantly put his slice down to cool, wiping his fingers on his napkin. "It's like molten lava. Tasty nuclear fusion. Seriously, though, what's the worst that can happen if the news gives us fifteen minutes of fame?"

Colleen shredded her napkin. "Fierocity could suffer."

"How?" he challenged.

"You're the media darling. They're going to make me out to be a bitch scheming to get into your pockets."

"Then they're missing the point. You could probably buy me three times over."

"Only two." She smiled at him and cut her pizza into bite-sized pieces.

"What the hell are you doing?" Chase glared at her plate, so appalled that she double-checked to make sure she wasn't slicing up puppies.

"What does it look like?" She used her knife and fork to pantomime cutting her food.

"You don't eat pizza with a knife and fork. You fold it. Like this." He demonstrated, taking a big bite. "Hot," he said fanning his mouth.

"It was the temperature of the sun a few moments ago. Did you think it had cooled off any in the meantime? I don't want to burn my fingers or have half of the cheese come off on my chin."

"Where's your sense of adventure?" he chided.

She blew on a piece and daintily forked it in her mouth. "I can eat mine now."

Chase made a face at her. Then put his pizza down while it cooled off some more. "So we've established that you're not after my money. How else could our relationship being in the press harm our careers?"

"What if someone starts digging?"

Chase shrugged. "I've got nothing to hide."

"I do," she said.

"Your past isn't a secret. They dredged that all up when you married Granger. It's old news."

"It still sells copies and ad clicks."

"That's because it's a beauty-and-the-beast story."

She was gripping her fork, about to stab him with it, when he said, "Hear me out."

"It better be good," Colleen warned him, and went back to her pizza instead.

"You're a breathtaking knockout with brains and balls. You married . . . well," he finished grudgingly. "You thrived as a widow. And you're powerful. You intimidate the hell out of most people, and the way little people deal with that is that they try to tear you down."

"Exactly, and by tearing me down, they'll tear down Fierocity and Couture."

Chase shook his head. "Not a chance. People want to be you more than they want to hate you. So as long as there's a Couture for them to aspire to or a hot new line to wear, you'll survive the storm."

"What about you? What if you shipwreck with me?"

"I'd love to be trapped on a deserted island with you." He lowered his voice and sent her a look of such sexual heat that it made the pizza ice cold in comparison.

"I can arrange that," she said.

"Are you going to import sand into the dungeon?"

"Maybe," Colleen laughed.

They finished their dinner. Chase waved to the family, who left before they did. Colleen's phone pinged.

It was a text from Nefertiti: *Check you out.*

"Tee has me on a Google alert," Colleen said at Chase's raised eyebrow.

The picture was an unflattering one. Chase was grinning

at her, but she had resting bitch face and her mouth was full. She showed him the picture.

"Nice tits," he said.

Typical. All he saw was her low neckline.

She read the website headline to him: "Fashion Maven Sinks Her Hooks into Football Hero."

"Those assholes." Chase half rose out of his chair, but she stopped him with a hand on his arm.

"It wasn't them. The angle on the picture is wrong. It came from the front of the restaurant."

"Let's get out of here before I start smashing phones." He threw a hundred on the table and helped her out of the booth.

"You should have let me pay. They're going to start with the gold-digging rumors next."

Chase wrapped his arm around her waist. "No way. You said this was my punishment, so it was my treat."

"Speaking of treats," Colleen said, "what kind of toys do you have back at your apartment?"

"I've got a bobble head of me in my away uniform." Chase thought for a moment. "A PS3. Why? You want to play Call of Duty?"

Colleen shook her head. "We're going to have to take a ride."

They didn't have to go back to Couture, but they did need a few things to enhance the evening. She guided him to the highway and told him what exit to get off at. The bright lights guided them down a very dark road to the twenty-four-hour sex shop.

"Shouldn't I be wearing my mask?" Chase said as he pulled the Mercedes into the empty parking lot.

"A little risk adds spice, don't you think?"

Chase hesitated.

Colleen crossed her arms over her chest, challenge in

every line of her body.

"You're the one who just got put on Tumblr with mozzarella in your teeth. What do you think the headlines are going to say if they upload a picture of us here?" Chase said.

He had a point. "Usually people don't take pictures in a shop they wouldn't want advertised they were in. However, you're right. I can't risk any connection to Club Inferno. So you're going in there on your own. Want me to make you out a list?"

"Any hard limits?" Now, it was his turn to challenge.

"Since you're going to be shopping for things I use on you, no. Not a one. Get what you like and make it good or I'll send you back in again."

"Yes, Mistress." He pulled her in for a rough kiss.

She was pleased to see he was getting hard. Rubbing the heel of her hand over the bulge in his pants, Colleen deepened the kiss. Chase cupped her breast, seeking out her nipple with his thumb. He circled the turgid peak, then plucked it hard.

Yeah, that was just how she liked it.

She undid his jeans and pulled his cock out. Without breaking off the kiss, Colleen felt him jolt in surprise when she climbed over the gear shift to straddle his lap. He eased back the seat as she was guiding him into her.

Chase's shout of surprise turned into a moan of pleasure in her mouth. The angle was wrong, so he couldn't be fully inside her. But it was enough. Chase fumbled under her skirt, grabbing on to the globes of her ass. She rode him with short, quick bounces. He tried to control the tempo, but the steering wheel was in the way. He shifted, but he was completely at her mercy.

Grinding her lips against his, she took him to the edge. He tried to say something, to turn his head to the side, but she held his face to hers and sucked on his tongue. Her body trapped his. He was too big to shift out from under her and it was too cramped for him to roll. It was better than restraints.

He moaned something, his body jerking and shaking. Chase's grip tightened on her ass, almost bruising. A moan broke out of her throat and Chase jerked free of her kiss.

"Coming," he told her.

"Ask permission." She gripped his hair, forcing him to make eye contact.

"Please." Chase gulped huge breaths. He shoved his hands up her blouse and tugged hard on her breasts.

"Oh yeah," Colleen moaned. "I was wondering if you forgot about them."

Chase's hips thrust upward, but he didn't have the leverage. A bead of sweat trickled down his forehead.

"Me first," she said.

Yanking up her shirt, Chase pulled her into him. His teeth grazed her nipple and she gasped. Her hips thrummed against him faster. He moaned his appreciation. "Please."

Colleen threw her head back and put her hands on the ceiling of the car. She watched Chase's eyes darken. He was so close. Her pussy clamped down hard on him.

"Baby," he groaned. "I can't stop."

She did it again as hard as she could.

"Fuck," Chase shouted. "Stop or I'll come."

"Not the words I want to hear."

"You're killing me," he ground out. "So damned sexy. Mouth made for sin. Those gorgeous breasts bouncing in my face." He maneuvered his hand between them. "And this?" He found her clit.

"Chase," she shrieked, unable to stop the fierce flood of desire from peaking at his rough caress. She squeezed him again.

"God." His head slammed back against the head rest. He worked his fingers fast, as he flooded his release inside her.

Colleen waited for the pang of disappointment, but even though he hadn't received permission to come yet, she was nearing her own orgasm. Chase looked at her with hooded eyes. He fingered her slowly now, letting her own bouncing rub his fingers against her. Chase went back to her breasts.

"I love . . ." He sucked a nipple hard into his mouth, swirling his tongue over the sensitive peak, while he managed to press on her clit.

Colleen's breath left her as shock pushed her into a blinding crash of jangled nerve endings.

" . . . these."

Now, the disappointment came as the ebbing tide of her orgasm slowly drifted away. Self-anger came next at being such an idiot. What had she thought he was going to say?

I love you.

He hadn't said that when they were together. He almost had. Once. But then he'd gotten a call from his buddies and the moment had been lost. Or maybe he had been going to say he loved her tits, just as he'd done just now. Who knew? Colleen climbed off him and settled herself into the passenger's seat. Chase pulled the seat back to the normal position and tucked himself in.

"Make sure you buy something for me to spank you with," she said, staring out the window while she composed her features. Colleen was proud her tone sounded even and firm.

"What for?" He trailed his finger up her arm.

"You didn't follow instructions."

"That's bullshit," he said. "That's entrapment."

Colleen felt a gurgle of amusement come up as she turned to face him. She could tell he wasn't sure whether to laugh or be outraged. "This isn't a court of law," she said. "It's my way or the highway, remember?"

"You cheated," Chase argued. "There's not a man alive who wouldn't go off like the Fourth of July with you on his dick. I'll whack your ass."

Colleen opened up the car door and walked out into the night. It was cold not wearing any underwear, but she had to treat Chase the way she'd treat any other submissive. No way in hell would she let them speak to her that way. Then again, they weren't in the dungeon. But she was his Mistress when they were having sex. That was the deal. Why was it so hard to keep things straight with Chase? Probably because it was all this old emotion—emotion that Colleen was beginning to realize wasn't as far in the past as she thought it was. She wasn't really angry. She wasn't sure what she was feeling. Colleen just knew she couldn't be in that car right now. Not when his admission of loving her was limited to her chest. Not when he thought he could switch from submissive to a half-assed dominant. Shivering, she rubbed her shoulders as she walked toward the road.

She heard the car door slam as Chase came after her.

Here comes the grenade.

"Where the hell are you going?"

And boom, the explosion.

Colleen didn't say anything. This was the cost of his disobedience. If he thought he could argue with his Domme, he had to be taught there were consequences. She usually thought the silent treatment was passive-aggressive, but in this case it worked. He caught up to her easily.

"Get your ass back in the car," he ordered.

Like that's going to work.

Chase just didn't get it. He was in big trouble. Trying to dominate the situation wasn't in his best interest. She kept on walking.

"What are you going to do? Hitchhike? I got news for you,

baby. I'll be reading about you in the papers tomorrow if you keep walking."

Colleen stopped and whirled around. "Are you threatening to call TMZ on me?"

"The fuck?" Chase asked. "I mean you're going to be a fucking statistic. There are bad men out there who would think it was Christmas, their birthday, and national blow job day all rolled up in one if they found you walking along a dark, deserted road."

"I can take care of myself." She wasn't going to hitchhike. She was going to call Istvahn to pick her up as soon as she found a place to stay that was safe enough to wait around in.

"Why are you throwing a tantrum?" he yelled.

"You're the one shouting like a maniac and throwing your arms around," she said calmly. "I decided to leave."

"Why? Because I'm not willing to play your little sex games?"

That hurt.

"You were willing enough when I was fucking you," she said with fake sweetness. Colleen wished she had something she could throw at his head.

"Why are we fighting?" he asked.

"I'm not fighting."

"If I go get a paddle, will you get back in the fucking car?"

Colleen considered it, and if it wasn't for the slight condescension in his voice she might have let that be the peace offering. But it was time she faced facts. The sex was amazing. Enough that she could overlook the lack of kink —for the time being. But in the long run she would become as resentful as he was now. "Chase, this isn't going to work."

"No. You don't get to say that every time it gets hard between us."

Her lips twitched. "It's always hard between us. And if

you get to throw my 'little sex games' at me every time your dick gets in a knot, it *isn't* going to work out between us."

Chase sighed, looking up at the sky for assistance.

"You're not a sub." Colleen shrugged. "We both know that. It was stupid to try."

"Why? Because I didn't get permission to come so hard that my head is still pounding? Both of them?"

"No," she said. "Only a trained sex slave could have stopped from coming at that point."

"I knew it." He pointed his finger at her. "You set me up."

"Yes. I wanted to see how you would react to failure. And how you would accept your punishment. Bravo." She did a slow golf clap.

Chase's jaw dropped.

"I found out all right." She turned back around. She was pretty sure there was a twenty-four hour Walmart down the road. Setting off, she regretted not wearing a sweater in addition to her underwear.

"My dad used to send me out to get a stick so he could hit me with it."

Shit. Colleen hung her head, caught between sadness and anger. She paused, weighing her next words carefully. "Then why did you choose spanking for your punishment?"

"I don't know." He ran his hand over his head. "You seemed to like it. And I'm a grown man. I should be over that. When I was all hot and bothered it didn't seem like such a big deal."

She could just kill him. "I told you not to do that. Not to pretend to want something because I want it."

"Give me a break." Chase shrugged out of his sweatshirt and jammed it over her head when she started to shiver again.

"Thank you." It was warm and smelled like him. She wrapped her arms around herself.

"I would crawl across glass to get you back. You can spank me if you want."

Damn it. This would be easier if he was a total asshat instead of a partial one. "Chase, I don't want to spank you if it hurts you emotionally as well as physically. If you have a daddy issue about it, it's not going to be good for either of us. I want sex between us to push the envelope, not make you feel like shit."

"I thought that's what all the hitting was all about. You get off on a big power trip."

Colleen counted to ten. The only thing saving him was that he wasn't being an asshole right now. He was being honest. Again, it was his lack of experience in the lifestyle. She took a deep breath. He wanted a teacher? Then she would instruct him. "I do get off on a big power trip. But it's not because I hurt someone when they're down. Some subs like pain. Some subs like humiliation. Some don't. Ignore the stereotypes and the caricatures. Everyone is an individual with different needs and desires. My job as a Domme is to find out what yours are and then push you to the limit of them. There are things I would do to and for another sub that I would never in a million years do with you."

"Why not?" he challenged.

Why is it always competition with him?

"Because you wouldn't like them. And if you wouldn't like it, neither would I."

"Are you saying Angie likes being beaten with a belt while giving head?"

"How do you know Angie?" Colleen put her hands on her hips.

"She introduced herself to me in the club last night. She sassed some guy who resembled Clark Kent with sleeve tattoos, and he hauled her over to a bald dude and forced her to her knees. I was going to stop it, but Anya told me not to bother. That it was a common enough occurrence."

Colleen nodded. "It sounds like Angie. And as long as the Dom she was sucking off wasn't Clint or Max, Anya was right. That's a typical day at Club Inferno. I'm pretty sure Angie was a deliberate pain in the ass until it got to that point, and then afterward everything was hunky-dory."

"It was like they beat her into submission."

"They did," Colleen said. "And she loved it. It's her kink. It's how she gets her limb-shaking, earth-shattering orgasms."

"She can come without all that stuff."

"How would you know?" Colleen snarled.

Chase held up his hands. "Whoa! Not by personal knowledge. Not that she didn't try to get me to go into the closet with her and play hide the salami."

Colleen's lips twitched. "Was Anya there when she was doing that?"

"She was, but she was taking bets on something with your secretary. I think it was on the pony race."

"Hmmm," Colleen said. She was pretty sure the money being exchanged was on whether Chase would tell Angie to pound sand or wind up pounding her on the sand.

"She's just obviously very sexual," Chase said. "So why would she need all the theatrics?"

"Why do you want sex when you can just jerk off? Why don't you just watch porn instead?"

"It's more fun with two people." Chase held up two fingers, then darted his tongue between them at her. He winked.

She ignored the sexual innuendo. "Exactly. It's more fun for Angie to play like this. I thought it would be more fun for you, but I'm beginning to see I was wrong."

"You don't want me without the leather mask?" Chase folded his hands in front of him.

"I do," she said.

His grin was so triumphant, she hated what she was going to say next. It was going to change everything. "But in the long run, I need the kink. Vanilla sex will only satisfy me for a short time. So I'm changing our exclusive relationship to an open one. You get to screw whomever you want, however you want. And so do I. We can be 'normal.'" Colleen finger-quoted the last word.

"That's not an option." The smile wiped from his face. "I don't want anyone else."

"It's the only option aside from us breaking up after two days."

He shook his head. "It's cold out here. You're freezing. Would you please get in the car? I'll drive you home, and we can finish this discussion where it's warm."

Colleen nodded. The fight had gone out of both of them, and she couldn't think of anything more depressing than hanging out in Walmart until Istvahn picked her up. "Take me back to Couture, though."

"Yeah," he said, and opened the car door for her. "I fucked it up again, didn't I?"

She waited until he slid back into the driver's seat and backed out of the parking lot. Colleen glanced wistfully at the sex shop's windows. So much potential wasted.

"I'm such an asshole," he said.

"Don't worry about it," Colleen said. "It wasn't meant to be."

His knuckles went white on the steering wheel.

"This permission thing gets you off, huh?" he grated out.

"The control does. It's who I am." She refused to argue with him anymore. It wouldn't solve anything.

"It didn't used to be like this." Chase stared straight ahead at the dark highway.

"People change." Colleen took off his sweatshirt and laid it across her lap. She turned on the heating vents full blast toward her. "Besides, there was always a wild dynamic to our lovemaking, even in Vegas."

"I want to make you happy," he said. "I want us to be together."

"You just don't want to be in the lifestyle where I dominate you sexually."

Chase shrugged. "I wouldn't say that. I kinda like it when you take initiative and boss me around."

"So what's the problem, then?" she asked, gesturing beseechingly at him.

"I'm just a dumb jock, baby. I'm not as complicated as you are."

"Oh, bullshit, Chase. You are the biggest complication in my life."

He cocked his head. "Is that a good thing or a bad thing?"

"If I was smart, I'd kick you out on your well-muscled ass. But I can't. I want this, too. I'm just not sure we can do it long-term."

"Don't give up on me yet," he said, reaching over to hold her hand.

"I'm trying to protect my heart." The honesty almost shattered her into a million pieces, and she wanted to grab those words back before he could twist them and use that emotion to hurt her.

He squeezed her hand and rubbed his thumbs across her knuckles. "What would have happened tonight if I had come back with a paddle and other things?"

Glancing out the window at the lights from the passing cars go by, she shrugged. "Depends. What would you have bought?"

"Handcuffs."

"What else?"

"Flavored lube."

Colleen smiled. "And?"

"Massage oil."

"Sounds like a good time. Anything else?"

"A vibrator I could use on you. Like the husband did with his wife in the prison cell dungeon."

Colleen sighed. They were still holding hands. "We would have started off in the shower, soaping each other up. I would have ordered you to make me come and then fuck me against the bathroom wall."

He swallowed hard.

"Then after we dried off, I would have ordered you to coat my body in the massage oil. It would have wrecked your sheets."

"Who gives a fuck?" he said hoarsely.

"I'd have handcuffed you to the bed or to a chair and dragged my slicked up body against yours until we were both coated. Then I'd use the flavored lube to lick off your hard cock and I'd suck on you until you were about to come. When you were about to explode, I'd spank you with the paddle. Ten hard shots. You would count them out. I'd judge your pain and arousal level and go back to sucking on you in between the smacks, until the pain faded to pleasure."

"Jesus." He let out a ragged breath.

"Then I'd fuck myself with the vibrator while you watched. After I came, I'd uncuff you and we would have sex until the body oil was rubbed completely off or until we fell asleep."

It was quiet in the car for many exits. "I had no idea," he said.

"You didn't trust me." Colleen tried for a shrug, but it hurt too much.

"I would have liked that."

"I know," she said in a monotone.

"Can I get a do-over?" He eyed her hopefully.

"Not tonight. The mood has been shot."

Chase nodded. "Are you going to go down to Club Inferno after I drop you off?"

"Probably."

His jaw tightened. "Are you going to pick up another sub to have sex with?"

"Not tonight. I have some work to do."

Chase sighed.

She inspected him out of the corner of her eye. It was obvious he didn't want her to go to the dungeon alone. And it was equally obvious he didn't like the thought that she was considering another lover. "I might observe, though. And if I find something or someone enticing . . ." She shrugged. "One thing could lead to another."

"I don't want to share you," he said quietly. It tore at her heart a little. Colleen wasn't onboard with sharing him, either.

"It's going to happen sooner or later. If we go into this relationship knowing that it's just a matter of time before we find someone else to fulfill all our needs, then we don't have to risk hurt feelings. We could still be friends."

"I don't want to be just your friend." Chase took his eyes off the road to stare at her. "I love—"

"My tits," she cut him off. "Yeah, so you've said."

"I love you," he said. "Do you think I would put up with this shit if I didn't?"

"You should have stopped at the first part." Colleen's heart was thudding loudly in her ears. Chase Fairwood loved her. All those thorns around her heart started shriveling up. She could see the truth on his face. "Sometimes love isn't enough," Colleen whispered in a small, hurt voice. "The shit will get to you after a while."

"It damn well is going to be enough," he told her. "You are not walking away from me after a fight and getting involved with another man. I'm not waiting another ten years. We're solving this problem and then we're heading toward a future together." Then Chase seemed to realize something, and his voice got soft and hurt. "That is, if you want one with me."

They drove on for a few more exits in silence. He passed the exit for Couture, but she didn't remind him.

"I'm changing the rules," she finally said.

Chase, for once, had the good sense to keep his mouth shut.

"Your punishment is abstinence."

A muscle in his jaw twitched.

"If you want out, just fool around with anyone else. I'll be as faithful to you as you are to me. But if you want something long-term with me, you keep your dick in your pants. Instead of spanking, as a punishment you don't get to fuck me or come. No masturbation, either—not unless I give you permission."

"What's the length of the punishment?" Chase said eagerly. "How long do I have to go without coming?"

Colleen was surprised that he didn't sound angry or resigned. "This time? One day," she said.

Some of the tension left his shoulders.

"I don't want to see you until the day after tomorrow." Colleen pulled her hand away. "And then you are to be dressed for the dungeon and waiting for me. I will be securing you to the chair for that session. I'll be using zip ties, so wear long sleeves and pants so the plastic won't cut into you. Again, you'll be an observer. You say one word during the workshop and you'll be abstaining for another day. You got that?"

"What's the catch?"

"No catch, Chase. The sex is supposed to be thrilling and

fun. It's not something to dread or balk at. If you didn't want to be spanked, you shouldn't have offered it."

He took a deep breath through his nose and blew it out. "Sorry," he said. "Now that you've explained it to me, I can see I was being an idiot again."

Colleen waved away his apology.

"Was this one of the awful things you were talking about?"

"It wasn't very fun," she countered.

"Yeah," he said, slinging his arm around her shoulder and giving her a quick hug and kiss on the head. "You don't need to protect your heart from me," he added.

Colleen stared up at him, wanting to believe.

"Look at it this way." He grinned down at her. "We worked this out better than the last time I flaked on you."

Colleen couldn't argue with that. Maybe they were learning. "Chase, this can't go the distance. You know that, right? This can only be temporary."

"Like you said, let's get through the first week before making any hasty decisions. Okay?"

Colleen rested her cheek on his shoulder. "Yeah."

They drove on like that until Chase's gas gauge lit up on empty. After he filled up the tank, he brought her back to Couture.

"Are we good?" He stopped her from getting out of the car with a hand on her arm.

"I think we're getting there."

"Can I kiss you good night?" he asked.

She shook her head.

"I should have bought the fucking paddle." He gave her a half smile.

"The night would've ended differently." Colleen got out of the car and closed the door. She forced herself not to look back at him.

CHAPTER 11

C hase watched Angie try to do biceps curls without whacking herself in the tits. He wanted to tell her not to try so hard. The people would be looking at her tank top and hoodie, not evaluating her lifting form.

"Haven't you gotten the shot yet?" she whined to Clint.

"Shut it," Clint barked at her.

Max crossed his arms in front of him. "Angie, do we have to take this to the dungeon?"

"No, Sir," she said meekly, but Chase could see a sparkle in her eye.

Here we go again.

Different strokes. He could see that Angie liked to cause trouble and was deliberately baiting both Clint and Max. Almost as if she was challenging them, daring them to punish her. So she got a kick out of being bossed around. Her nipples were drawn out tight against the sports bra. He noticed, but it didn't do a thing for him. Not when Colleen was only a floor and a half above him, probably dressed in a Chanel suit with fuck-me lingerie underneath it.

He had to stop thinking so much. It got him in trouble all

the time. He really should just do what Colleen said in the bedroom. He wanted to please her. He wanted to be her man. It was just going to take some getting used to. That was all.

His phone vibrated on the seat next to him. Checking it, he saw it was from Kevan Lewis, one of his old teammates who hadn't made it to the fashion show. Catching Max's attention, Chase indicated that he'd be right back, and stepped out into the hallway.

"Kevan, what's shakin'?" Chase said, his voice lowered because he'd left the door to the studio ajar just in case they finished with Angie sooner than expected. It looked like he had a few minutes, though. Clint had Angie posing with one knee on the workout bench doing triceps pulls. Angie was wiggling her butt as if daring Clint or Max to whack it.

"Tell me this shit was Photoshopped," Kevan said.

"This shit was Photoshopped," Chase replied dutifully. "What are we talking about?"

"I'm sending it to you now."

Flicking his finger over the phone, he opened up the attachment Kevan just sent. It was a picture from the pizzeria last night.

"Tell me that's another blonde and not the one who broke your balls and married the geezer from Texas."

A twinge of annoyance edged into Chase's voice. "Colleen and I are back together."

"Oh man, you've got to be kidding me. For how long? Until she finds another sugar daddy?" Kevan's voice was full of derision.

"She's not like that," Chase broke in, but Kevan just rolled right over him.

"She's still hot, though. Can't say I blame you. I'd go back for a second tap at that ass."

"Watch it," he growled.

"Easy, killer. Does she still like to play dress-up and play with whips?"

"None of your business."

"She does! Holy shit, that's hot. She got any friends?"

Chase had to laugh. "You should come down to Couture the next time you're playing New England. Her dance club is off the hook."

"I'll take you up on that, man. The boys said it was all swank and sweet young thangs looking for a good time."

They don't know the half of it.

Because Kevan hadn't been at the fashion show with the rest of his old teammates, he'd missed seeing Couture and the Hot Spot. At least he had a good excuse: his daughter had graduated from high school.

"They didn't tell me you were back with the ice bitch, though."

The fact that Kevan would even think of calling Colleen an ice bitch was proof he had no idea what she was like. Still, Chase needed to call him out. "Back off my woman, or I'm going to shove my foot so far up your ass, your breath is going to smell like my gym socks."

Kevan guffawed in his ear. "Bring it, gimp."

Chase figured it was too much to hope for that they would let this drop. It would probably be better if he said this to all of them in person. While Kevan talked some more good-natured trash, Chase brought up the team's schedule on his phone. They had the Thursday night game next week at Giants Stadium. "I can be in Jersey for the game. If you guys are free, we can hang out."

"Just like old times. I'll ring you with the hotel information. Bring your arm candy and some of her girlfriends."

Chase gave a nervous laugh. "Colleen's got other plans. But we'll plan for something with all of us soon."

Yeah, that was all he needed. He wouldn't have sex for a

year if he subjected Colleen to those bozos without warning them off.

"I get it. Still a bachelor at heart."

"It's not like that."

"Don't worry, dawg, there's plenty of pussy to go around. Stay for the game. Coach would love to have you on the sidelines."

"Wouldn't miss it." Chase shook his head as Kevan rang off.

I'll be as faithful to you as you are to me.

His playing days were over—both on the field and off.

When he came back in the room, it was just Angie. She was changing into another outfit.

"Shit," Chase said. "Sorry."

Angie turned around. Chase swallowed. A natural redhead. He was pretty sure Max didn't design women's underwear, but Angie had decided not to wear any.

"It's okay. I like showing off."

Chase peeked out the door, hoping for someone, anyone to be there to rescue him. "This isn't the club," he said. "Anyone could walk in on you."

"I know," she said. "I like the thrill. Want me to blow you while Master Clint and Master Max are getting the next set ready?"

"No, thanks. That's all right." Chase put one foot in the hallway and desperately searched for the two men.

"They'll be another ten minutes or so. The next set is probably going to be in their dojo."

"I should go," he said.

"You can fuck me. I'm already wet. I've got a condom, too, if you're worried. I like it hard and fast. You can pull my hair and slap my ass."

"I need to go. It's not you. It's me. I'm in a relationship." Chase was babbling. If Kevan could see him now, he'd be all over him for being pussy-whipped. But the fact of the matter was he could have all the Angies he wanted. Hell, a few years ago he would've been all over the free blow job and the quick bang between takes. As stunning as Angie was—and he checked her out, he wasn't dead—it wasn't worth losing this shot with Colleen. Now, if it'd been Colleen naked making those offers, he'd have already come.

"Thanks, though. I'm flattered." He started to close the door.

"Just go." Angie waved a bored hand at him.

Colleen did a double take when she walked into her office. Jana was behind Nefertiti's desk.

"She wasn't feeling well," Jana said by way of greeting. "Master Dante said I should fill in."

Looking her over critically, Colleen nodded in approval at the Valentino crepe dress Jana wore. It was cut low in the front, but the colors and style fit Jana's personality, so it rode the edge of fashion. It was acceptable office wear. At least at Couture.

"Thank you. Would you page Istvahn and tell him I'd like to see him if he's not with Nefertiti?"

"Yes, Ma'am."

She made a mental note to thank Dante for his quick thinking. A paranoid part of her niggled in the back of her brain that this was his way of trying to get control. But the more civilized portion acknowledged that it was a professional courtesy, and a nice thing to do.

Colleen sauntered into her office. She had to come up with something for this month's staff development program, but she had nothing. She had wasted a lot of time on the Chase situation, and she needed to have a plan in place for Friday's meeting. If it came down to it, Colleen supposed, they could always have an eighties night and do hot-oil wrestling. Groaning, she rested her head on her desk.

That idea sucked.

Her intercom buzzed, and she straightened up. "Yeah?"

"Anya Litton here to see you."

"Send her in."

Anya breezed in, closing the door behind her.

"Since when do you need to be announced?" Colleen asked as Anya went over to the bar and grabbed some cherries and fruit slices on a paper napkin.

"I figured we weren't friends anymore because you haven't said a freaking word about your new sex slave to me." Anya chewed on an orange and slumped into the chair opposite her desk.

"Chase and I are taking it slow."

"I saw homeboy with a ski mask on. Are you going to collar him, too?"

Colleen rolled her eyes. "Yeah, like that would go over well."

"Just flex those Domme muscles of yours." Anya pumped up and flashed her biceps, nearly spilling a lemon on the floor.

"Chase is different. He's new to all of this. It's kind of refreshing to see everything through a newbie's perspective. If I wanted absolute obedience, I'd negotiate with Dante for Jake."

"So, are you going to dish on what you've been doing in the dungeons all this time?"

"You mean this week?" Had it only been just a few days? She really should cut Chase some slack.

Anya nodded. "Spill it."

"He's coming along nicely."

"Oh, I bet he is," Anya said, and then sobered. "Are you happy?"

Colleen fought a smile, and then let it shine through. "It's been a pretty rough twenty-four hours. But I'm optimistic."

"Take it one day at a time, then."

"I plan to."

"Have you checked your email yet?" Anya switched to the cherries.

"I just walked in. Is there something I should be aware of?"

Anya's lips twitched. "Open it up."

"It better not be a link to someone's sex tape. I get so upset when I know our video production quality is superior." Colleen called up her email, skimming over the usual spam and notices. But one name caught her attention. She put a hand over her heart that was threatening to beat out of her chest. "That's the head editor for *La Femme Actuelle*."

"Just the biggest fashion magazine in France. Vogue can suck it." Anya rubbed her hands together gleefully.

Colleen's hands shook a bit as she read the email. "'We would be pleased to feature the Fierocity line in one of our upcoming features.' *Putain de merde!*"

"It didn't say that last part."

"No, that was all me. They want to interview us and do a photo shoot in Calais." Colleen's mouth dropped open.

"Isn't that fantastic?" Anya screeched, and slapped a high five on Colleen's palm.

"Who are we sending to monitor the shoot? Marisol? Does she speak French?"

"I'm going, and so are you," Anya said.

"I can't get away right now. I'm worried about Nefertiti. But you go and take Marisol with you. I'll get you set up with a company credit card, and Jana can make the arrangements for you."

"Hot damn!" Anya did a little jig.

"I need Clint here, though."

A little air went out of her sails. "Are you sure?"

"We need to get Club Inferno's pay website off the ground."

"He can do that from France," Anya wheedled.

"I need him here."

"Okay," Anya capitulated. "But it's going to cost you a Lancel purse."

"Deal," Colleen said.

"I'll go pack." Anya danced out of her office, narrowly missing treading all over Istvahn's toes.

"You wanted to see me?" he asked, standing at parade rest in front of her desk.

"How's Tee doing?"

Concern and frustration flashed over his features, and if Colleen hadn't known him so well, she probably would have missed it completely. "Her blood pressure is elevated. She has a doctor's appointment later on today. I'm hoping he'll put her on strict bed rest for the rest of her pregnancy. I don't like the way her ankles are swelling."

"The glucose test came back okay," she reminded him.

He gave her a curt nod.

"You do whatever you have to do," Colleen said. "Don't worry about a thing here. I have Chase with me. He can double as a bodyguard if it's needed." Seeing Istvahn begin to object, she added quickly, "And it won't be needed."

"He's still in the catalog shoot," Istvahn said.

Colleen looked over at the clock. "That's going on longer than I expected it to."

"From what I gathered, Angie needed to be disciplined, and that set them behind schedule."

"Angie?"

Her voice must have been louder than she had planned, because Istvahn's eyebrows also rose. "I believe after Max and Clint warned her to stop fooling around, they called in Steve to instruct her on the error of her ways."

"What was Chase doing?"

Istvahn lifted a shoulder. "I think he was playing on his phone."

Colleen tried for nonchalant. "Were there a lot of shots with them together?"

"There was one where he was bench-pressing her."

"Really?" Colleen pressed her lips together.

"You want me to keep him under surveillance?"

She waved her hand. "No, I've got enough things to worry about. If I can't trust him alone with Angie, I'd better find out now."

Istvahn nodded.

"Still, she'd think he was a challenge and would go all out to get him."

Istvahn remained silent.

"Go check on Tee for me. Tell her I sent you. Bring her some chicken soup from the deli."

"And some half-sour pickles," he said.

"And some Ben and Jerry's."

"No," Istvahn said. "I don't want her to have too much sugar."

Colleen smiled at his mother hen attitude. "Keep me updated," she said.

"On Tee or Chase?"

"Both."

Istvahn nodded, turned on his heel, and left. Dante sauntered in shortly after.

It's like Grand Central station this morning.

Dante closed the door and locked it behind him.

This ought to be good.

"What can you do for me, Dante?" Colleen asked, deliberately playing around with the wording of a typical greeting.

"I live to serve." He bowed.

"I'll believe that when I see it."

"May I sit?"

Colleen indicated the chair in front of the desk. It was the same one Chase had sat in a few nights earlier. She leaned back in her chair and crossed her legs. Dante lost focus for a moment, staring at her legs. She let the silence stretch, glaring hard at him until he met her eyes again.

"What's the staff development meeting going to be this week?"

"It's a surprise," Colleen bit out, defensive in spite of herself.

"I had some thoughts."

"Nothing's set in stone yet." This would be great. One less thing to worry about, plus it would give her more time to prepare Anya and Marisol for the France trip. And with Nefertiti out she could really use a break in her schedule.

"Why don't we transform Club Inferno into a circus?"

Colleen made a face. "You and your acrobats do that shtick every night anyway. How would this help the staff?"

"I figured we could dress up. You and I could be the ring-masters. The staff could try their hands at screwing on the high wire or on the trapeze."

Colleen smiled. "No, not a circus. A carnival."

"We could set up the rooms like Rio de Janeiro and have a masked costume ball."

"Meh," Colleen said. "It's been done. Besides, Carnivale was in February. It's almost June. Anyway, I meant a carnival as in a Ferris wheel and midway games."

Dante snapped his fingers. "I like that. We could have sexual favors as prizes instead of stuffed animals."

"I'll tell you what. You can be in charge of the staff development. You have a modest budget. Don't go crazy."

"You mean it?" He leaned forward.

She'd show Anya she wasn't a control freak. "It's all yours."

"You won't regret it."

The intercom buzzed. Jana's disembodied voice said, "Chase Fairwood to see you."

"I don't want to see him until tomorrow." Colleen really did want to see him, but it was part of his punishment. She wondered if he'd hit up Angie for dinner that night.

Dante's grin grew even wider. "Well, I have a lot of work to do." He got up from his chair and unlocked the door. "Thank you, Mistress," he said as he opened the door. "Your trust in me won't be misplaced. I will do everything in my power to please you."

Colleen waved him away. He was putting it on a little thick.

"I will be at your beck and call. If you need me tonight, you only have to summon me."

He gave her a low bow and disappeared.

She rolled her eyes at his theatrics.

CHAPTER 12

Chase wasn't going to say a fucking word. Even though he had a lot of things he wanted to talk with Colleen about. For starters, that smarmy bastard Dante was just begging for Chase's foot up his ass, and not in a pain-is-pleasure sort of way. But if Chase uttered a single syllable, the punishment was another day of abstinence. He hadn't thought that meant he wouldn't be seeing Colleen, just that they wouldn't be doing the wild thing on her desk.

He stared at her. She wasn't dressed in leather this time. Colleen had on a 1950s housewife outfit, complete with apron and pearls. Her hair was held back from her pretty face with a wide, matching headband. She was dressed like June Cleaver, if you didn't look too closely at her shoes. The stilettos gave her away. He'd also bet his 401(k) that she was wearing a garter belt and silk stockings under that dress.

"Don't make me ball-gag you," she had warned him when she walked into the dungeon, which was set up like a small kitchen and family room. His chair was in the den, and the way everything was decorated reminded him of his nana's old house. There was even plastic on the furniture. Colleen pointed to his chair. No kiss. No fondle. Just a hard shove into the chair where, true to her word, she trussed him up with plastic restraints and then ignored him.

The only thing that was stopping him from mouthing off was the fact that she looked as grumpy as he felt. She actually seemed a little nervous. Colleen never let anyone see her sweat. He started to get a bad feeling about this.

The door was thrown open and a middle-aged couple walked in. The man was the one who had cock-blocked him at the Fierocity show, Senator Clemmons. He shut the door to the dungeon while a woman Chase assumed was his wife click-clacked her sensible heels over to Colleen.

"So, at last I meet my husband's Mistress."

Chase heard the capital M in her voice.

Colleen inclined her head.

"If you think you're going to steal my husband so you can marry another powerful man, you have another thing coming to you, you little whore."

Chase shifted in his chair. The bindings on his arms and legs were too tight to get out of. He was going to kick Grandma in her ass if she didn't knock it the hell off.

"Take a look at what's sitting in that chair." Colleen pointed her chin at him.

Chase froze when the harpy turned around to glare at him with beady black eyes.

"I have my own money," Colleen said. "My own power. And I fuck him every night."

Not last night, Chase thought sourly.

"Why would I need or want your husband?" Colleen challenged, crossing her arms in front of her.

The tight-faced sourpuss gave him a once-over, and her lustful glance made him a little uneasy. He didn't want to think about what Dante had said to him over a beer at Cielie's last night. Chase hadn't expected him to invite him out for a drink, but since Colleen wasn't taking his calls and he wanted to know just what the hell Dante had been talking about on his way out of her office, Chase had been game to go to the Irish pub at Couture with him.

Over corned beef sandwiches, Dante told him more about what a sub could expect in the dungeons of Club Inferno. Like being shared with whomever his Domme chose to give him to. Chase didn't believe that Colleen would go against what they had originally talked about. Yet she seemed eager to make their relationship an open one. He was going to safeword all over the place if the senator's wife put a claw on him—even if it cost him another day of abstinence.

But the nasty old crow just eye-fucked him and then turned back to Colleen. "You want a shot at the White House."

This bitch didn't know Colleen at all.

Colleen smirked. "Not as First Lady. And since my past would be political suicide to any party willing to endorse me, that's not going to happen."

"So if you're not after my husband or my position, and you claim not to be fucking him, what the hell are you doing here every Thursday?"

"I'm so glad you asked."

Please. Oh, please. Chase did not want to see the senator's wrinkly old ass have sex. But as luck would have it, he didn't have to. Clemmons bent over the Formica kitchen table and pulled down his pants. As luck would have it, Chase's vision was blocked by the vinyl tablecloth.

"Martin, what are you doing?"

Chase cocked his head. Grandma didn't sound surprised or outraged. There was a breathy excitement in her voice. Glaring at Colleen, he wondered if this was an elaborate scene instead of reality. Colleen walked to a pantry-type cabinet and pulled out a rattan cane.

"He's being punished."

Colleen wound up and spanked Clemmons's ass five times. Chase only flinched at the first crack of wood hitting skin. He toughened up and watched as the worries dropped from the senator's face. There was a serene bliss after Colleen finished the last shot.

"I think you should give him more." The wife was a little bloodthirsty.

"He has to ask nicely," Colleen said in a deadpan voice.

"Please, Mistress. I've been so naughty. Please give me more."

"Not me. Her." Colleen pointed to his wife.

"Misty, please spank me."

"Well, I don't know," Misty said, but she was already rolling up her sleeves and heading over to her husband.

"Not your hand," Colleen ordered. "He doesn't deserve that." She went into the pantry again and pulled out a small pizza peel. "Use this instead."

Colleen yanked on the senator's head. "I want to hear you count." She dropped his head when he nodded. "Twenty should suffice. Hard as you can."

Misty wound up and swung like the bases were loaded at Yankee Stadium.

Chase only wished Colleen could see his expression under the leather mask. He was anti-hard. In fact, it would have been more stimulating to watch paint dry. Colleen showed Misty a better technique to swing the paddle with. She mastered the loud crack enough that the noise didn't bother Chase.

Sauntering back over to him while the senator choked out his punishment, Colleen leaned in and spoke in his ear. "Clemmons is an old client of mine. He likes the spankings. Which reminds me . . ." Colleen shouted back to Clemmons, "You are not allowed to come. If you do, I will chain you to the sofa and you will not get free until your wife comes five times."

"Five?" Misty gasped, and redoubled her efforts.

"He'll never last." Colleen went back to whispering in his ear. "He's afraid that if he doesn't come right away, he won't be able to later. We've been working on delayed gratification, but he comes immediately when I'm working on him."

I wonder why. Chase rolled his eyes. The old pervert had good taste.

True to her word, the senator gave up the ghost around seventeen. Chase would never have believed it if he hadn't seen it himself. Apparently some people really did get off on the pain.

"I'm ashamed of you. You only had three more to go." Colleen grabbed Clemmons by the collar and tossed him on the plastic couch. Pulling out handcuffs, she showed Misty the specially built rings to attach him to.

While Misty rigged her husband up, Colleen opened the door and whistled. A shirtless male sub came in. Chase hated him on sight. He was young and pretty, with long black hair that made women go crazy. Built like a stripper, the sub dropped to his knees at Colleen's feet.

Watch it, buddy.

"Hello, Jake," she said.

Chase bit back a snarl at the last minute. He tensed his wrists against the bindings. She had said he couldn't say a word. She hadn't said he couldn't get out of his restraints. Dante had told him that Jake was the man Colleen had wanted for a lover. If she thought that he would sit by while another man put his hands on her, Chase would show her that it wasn't on today's agenda. But the ties held firm.

"What is thy bidding, Mistress?" Jake lowered his gaze.

Give me a break.

"I need to attend to matters. You will see to it that my guests have everything they need."

"Everything?" Misty said with a hand on her heart.

"Everything." Colleen jerked Jake's chin up and looked him dead in the eyes. "Do you understand?"

"I live to serve, Mistress. Thank you."

She gave Jake a tap on the cheek that was more of a slap than a caress. "Help Misty in whatever she desires."

"Anything I desire?" Misty said faintly.

"Five." Colleen held up her palm in front of Clemmons's face, who was blinking out of the haze of arousal the caning and paddling had put him in. "If you can't do it, Jake will show you what you're doing wrong."

"Oh my," Misty gasped.

"But I'm tied down," the senator said. "I can't move."

"That's right." Colleen smirked. "It's time to pay for your orgasm. She will use you like a sex toy. And you'd better be a good one, because if you're not, you get to watch Jake make your wife scream in pleasure."

Misty actually sagged into a chair next to the couch. Jake knelt at her feet with his head down. "Command me and I will obey," he said.

So Dante had been right. The subs were shared. If that was the case, though, shouldn't Chase be the one on his knees in front of the harpy? Jake didn't seem to be upset that he would be using his skills not on Colleen but rather on an older woman whom he couldn't possibly find attractive. Or did he? Chase saw Jake shiver when Misty petted his hair.

"I'll be back in an hour to check on you. Misty, if your husband finishes with you before I get back, you can spank him some more."

The senator brightened up at that.

"But stick with the paddle or your hand. The cane takes practice, and we'll go over that next week."

"Thank you, Mistress," she said, still playing with Jake's hair.

Flipping open a butterfly knife, Colleen cut the zip ties holding Chase down. He was up and out the door like a shot, not wanting to see what came next. He realized that he wasn't sure where they were going, so he slowed down to wait for Colleen.

Colleen had cut it short with the Clemmonses because she had noticed that Chase was beginning to look a little green under the mask. She hadn't meant to upset him, but she wanted him to see a different view of discipline than the one he'd seen in the audience at Miranda's Midnight House of Pain. Reaching down for his hand, she grasped it and tugged him along the back corridors. The club's workshops were in session, but Colleen didn't want to dawdle. She had missed him last night, and she was planning on making up for lost time.

Taking him through a few doors that only she and Istvahn knew were there, Colleen pressed her fingertip to the scanner in her private elevator. Chase stood perfectly still as the car shot up several floors in scant seconds. She wondered if she had gone too far, bringing him to today's workshop. But when she tried to let go of his hand, he tightened his fingers and gave her a sexy smile. Colleen relaxed. He was still playing his part, that was all. As the doors opened up into her penthouse apartment, above the club and above Couture, she said, "You may get comfortable and speak."

The first thing Chase did was toss off the mask. "I really hate that thing."

"It was either that or have the senator know who was watching him."

"Good point." Chase rubbed his face. "So I'm forgiven?"

"You did very well with your punishment. I'm impressed."

"It's certainly a deterrent." He grabbed her in his arms and pulled her in for a rough kiss.

Rational thought fled as she relaxed in his arms. She'd never get tired of his mouth on hers. Sliding her hands under his T-shirt, Colleen stroked the wide plane of his back. "It was almost as hard on me as it was for you," she said when they took a breath.

"Maybe we should come up with another punishment?" Chase dipped his head and nibbled on her throat.

Colleen cupped her palm and gave him a hard whack on his ass.

Chase grunted and hauled her in closer. "Okay," he said.

"We'll see." She captured his mouth again as he yanked up her dress. Colleen moaned when he cupped his hands over her ass.

"I like it when you wear a garter belt." Chase tugged on it. "If you leave it on, I think that might scour the image of Helen Mirren paddling Anthony Hopkins out of my head."

Colleen shimmied out of his grip and unbuttoned her dress. "Is that all you can say about what you saw?"

"Not in a million years are you going to spank me over a Formica table."

Colleen laughed and let her dress fall to the ground. She stepped over it. "There's beer in the fridge if you want it," she called over her shoulder as she moved deeper into the apartment. "What I want to know is, can you now see the difference between sex and discipline?"

Trailing clothing with each step, Colleen worked on the tough girdle. It was vintage and stood up to a lot of abuse. She sighed in satisfaction when it came free.

"I do," he said from the kitchen.

Colleen heard the fridge open and the pop of the can. She was naked except for her pearls, garter belt, and stockings. She heard Chase prowling around behind her, but she didn't glance back until she was flat on her back on her king-size bed.

He leaned a shoulder against the doorway and stared at her. He took a deep pull from the bottle. "That dungeon scene had to be the most anti-sexy thing I've ever seen. You, however . . ." The hand that wasn't holding the beer bottle unbuttoned his pants.

"My objective wasn't to turn you on but to educate you."

"I get it," he said. "I'll pass on the senator's future sessions if you don't mind."

"I thought it was good for you to see that he ejaculated from the act of being caned and paddled. When he's with me, he's not supposed to come. But the old fool does it anyway. I punish him for it, of course, and then he has to explain his bruises and soreness to his wife."

"So she was on board with all of this? That was all an act."

Colleen played with the strand of pearls while she thought about it. "A lot of people speak the truth under the guise of role play. It's passive-aggressive, but sometimes that's what it takes."

"So she really did think you were fucking that toad?"

"I'm sure it crossed her mind. It never crossed mine."

"Why not?" Chase asked.

"You mean he's younger than Alfie and has a line on the presidency?"

"Those were her words. I'm curious. And you've never been fazed by age or looks."

Colleen spread her legs and moved her hand down between them.

Chase finished his beer as he stepped into the room. He put it on the top of her bureau.

"When you look like me, you get firsthand knowledge of how superficial beauty really is. One of the most thrilling men I ever met could make me come just by ordering it."

Chase cringed. "Let me guess. You married him."

"Wouldn't you?"

He laughed and then blinked in surprise. "Can you teach me to do that?"

"Chase, that's my ultimate goal."

"Well, all right." He lifted his shirt over his head. "Wait, did you mean make me come just by ordering it or that I make you come?"

"Why don't you stick around and find out?" Colleen parted the folds of her pussy and stroked the glistening bud she revealed to him.

Yeah, that got his attention. It was always more fun when someone watched. Biting her lip, she crooked her finger at him.

"Is this another one of your dungeons?" he asked, sitting down on the corner of the bed. He licked his lips like he wanted to be where her fingers were.

"This is my apartment." Colleen was growing wetter as he watched.

"What's the scene?" Chase kicked off his shoes.

She glanced at the clock. "We have an hour until I have to get back to the Clemmonses. We can do whatever you want for fifty-five minutes. I need the remaining five to get dressed and get back to the dungeon."

Chase pulled down his underwear and pants. "Anything I want?" he repeated. "So I can spank *you*?" The bed dipped as he climbed on it and crawled toward her.

Colleen nodded. "You expressed an interest the other night. You got to see a nonsexual version of it today. With a few guidelines, we can work it into our play. You'll spank me the way I want you to, though." She flicked her fingers faster as he pressed a kiss to her inner thigh. He bit her, a soft nibble that nearly sent her over the edge.

He moved up next to her, leaning up on his side. She

could feel the heat from his body, but they weren't touching. Not yet.

"Or I could pin your ankles above your head and fuck you hard until you come?"

"Please do," Colleen said, extending her leg up.

"I could also turn on the television and watch reruns of Sunday night football and eat Cheetos." Chase tugged on her pearls, his knuckles brushing the underside of her breasts.

"I would remind you don't need me for one of those choices." Her breath was coming in short pants, and still he just watched.

"Oh, I need you all right." He inched his face closer to hers. "Only an hour, right?"

"Fifty-three minutes."

"I'd better get to it then."

"You'd better," she had a chance to murmur before he brushed his lips over hers—once, twice, three times, each kiss a little longer than the last. His mouth was warm and his tongue demanding.

Chase propped himself up on an elbow. Trailing his fingertips down her body, he traced the edge of her stockings. "You are the most beautiful woman, I have ever seen." He blew softly across her breasts.

Colleen's nipples, already puckered, tightened. She bit her lip and opened her thighs, straining her chest toward him. Chase stared into her eyes. There was something in them that she wasn't expecting. She saw desire, a deeper emotion the trembling in her stomach recognized as love, and mischief.

Mischief?

"I want to talk."

"Talk?" Colleen balked, stopping the sweet rub on her clit. She pushed his shoulders until he was on his back.

159

She straddled his hips, put her hands on his chest and leaned down at him. "You're kidding, right?"

"We only have fifty-one minutes. Baby, that's not enough time to do everything I want to do to you." He flipped her over.

Colleen huffed in frustration. She had figured after a day of forced abstinence, Chase would be inside her already. Still, she liked getting a taste of her own medicine. Cuddling up against him, she stroked his hip and the curve of his fine, muscled ass. Two could play at that game. Dotting kisses along her jaw, Chase inhaled sharply as her hand might have dipped to tease the head of his cock.

"Of course, tonight I plan on fucking you in every way imaginable," he growled in her ear. "If that pleases you, Mistress."

She gasped when his fingers plunged inside her. Wet and aching, she met his thrusting fingers with her hips.

"You please me," Colleen said, gripping his cock.

He groaned. "Are you sure you can't let those two in the dungeon find their own way out?"

Colleen wished she could. Especially when he rubbed the velvet tip of his cock against her hip. "They pay me a lot of money to guide them." But they had plenty of time still. At least forty-eight minutes. Colleen pumped him in time to the rhythm his fingers were drilling into her.

Their mouths tangled again. Her angle was wrong so she couldn't jerk off fast and rough, not with him pressed tight against her.

"Chase, please," she cried raggedly when his mouth left hers to suck hard on her nipple. "God."

Pleasure crashed into her and she came all over his fingers. Pulling her hand away, he moved between her thighs and replaced his fingers with his cock.

"Yes," Colleen rested her thighs on his chest, so he went deeper.

Chase paused there, rammed in to the hilt. He gripped her legs roughly before moving his hands down her body. Rocking gently, Chase massaged her breasts until she was panting, his touch loving and wild. He pounded into her, making her breasts sway with each hard push. Teeth gritted, he asked, "Mistress, may I come?"

She shook her head wordlessly.

He increased the pace. The bed creaked loudly, a sound that made her toes curl. He fucked her harder, with quick, little strokes instead of the bed-shaking long ones.

"Mistress, may I come?" Chase's voice was strained, desperate.

Colleen barely got out the word "No" before her ankles were pinned by her ears and all she could feel was Chase's cock drilling into her, deep, hard, relentless.

"Yes," she cried. "Oh yes."

"Colleen," he roared.

She saw bright lights and her body purred and hummed. So close. She shouted his name with each thrust that slammed into her. Colleen's pussy spasmed around his cock. "Come, my love. Come for me," she said.

With an inarticulate grunt that bordered on panic, Chase let go. His fingers left marks on her thighs as he came.

"Mine," he said as his breath came back. "And only mine." Without slipping out of her, he eased them back to a more comfortable position on the bed.

When their heartbeats came back to normal, Colleen checked the clock. She had about ten minutes. She spent five of them kissing Chase, which was becoming her favorite pastime.

"I thought you wanted to talk," she said against his mouth.

"Talking is overrated," he replied. "I usually wind up

fucking something up." He hugged her closer. "I want this. I want you."

Her heart skipped giddily. "Even if you don't always like or get what I'm doing?"

"I get that you have a plan," he said, touching her temple. "I'm willing to let go and let you take me on a ride."

She buried her face in his chest. "It means so much to me that you said that."

He stroked her back. "I'm not perfect. You and I are going to tangle a lot. But there's no place I'd rather be right now. I might not understand the kink, or maybe what floats someone's boat sinks mine, but in the end, as long as I'm with you I can handle it. You and only you," he emphasized.

"You and only you," she agreed.

CHAPTER 13

⚜

Colleen's first thought when she walked into the staff development meeting in the party room of Club Inferno was that she should have monitored Dante a little more closely. Instead of the sexy carnival midway she had been expecting, he had turned it into casino night. A casino with a decidedly circus theme.

"I have a ringmistress costume for you," Dante said, gesturing to the changing rooms. "And you can decide what costume you'd like your sub to wear. We have a lion's costume and an elephant's one in his size."

"Did he just call me fat?" Chase asked when Dante walked away.

"You don't have to wear an animal costume if you don't want. You'd have to crawl on your hands and knees."

"What about the tail-in-my-ass thing?"

Well, that's new. "Sure, you can just wear that."

"No." Chase came to a dead stop. "That's not what I meant." He pantomimed a football penalty. Colleen wasn't sure if it was unnecessary roughness or offsides. Either way, she thought it was cute.

"Why don't you stick to what you're wearing now?" She patted his arm affectionately. They'd work up to anal play. Chase didn't seem to mind the outfit he wore ever since they'd switched out the full leather mask with a half face mask that left his nose and mouth clear.

The ringmistress outfit Dante had set aside for her was hanging on a peg with her name on it. Colleen put on the fishnet stockings, black shorts with a flap over the crotch for easy access, and the red bustier. Everything fit perfectly. She was going to assume Nefertiti had given Dante her sizes; otherwise she'd have to think about recruiting Dante for more fashion projects. The outfit was completed with a top hat, a black jacket with tails, and a signal whip rolled up on her hip.

Chase liked it, if his wide grin was anything to go by. She grabbed a handful of his T-shirt and brought him down for a kiss that left them wanting more.

"Come on, let's do the rounds and see if we can make it an early night," she said.

While a Las Vegas theme never would have been her first choice, Colleen had to admit that Dante had done a really good job with authenticity. The subs were behind the games of chance, like blackjack, craps, and, from the looks of it, strip poker. Everyone seemed to be having a fun time, and that was the point of the staff development. Work and play sometimes mixed, so play became work. When the dungeon staff got together like this, it was all about support and letting go of any other expectations except pleasure. Tonight the Doms and Dommes had a night off and were clients, just like the subs who volunteered to "work" tonight were.

"I like the naked croupiers," Colleen said to Chase.

"Now if I said that, I'd get smacked."

"Keep staring at Angie and you'll know the definition of smacked," Colleen warned.

"I'm not staring—much."

Angie finger-waved at him. She was a blackjack dealer tonight. Her heavy breasts almost dusted the table.

"At least you know they don't have anything up their sleeves."

"Up their *sleeves*," Colleen emphasized, "no. But that buzzing isn't the lights."

"Good to know," he said, sliding his fingers into hers.

They took a stroll around the casino floor. It felt incredibly familiar. Only this time her boss wasn't nattering in her earpiece to take Chase to the sports bar and have him do shots of tequila off her cleavage.

The betting just wasn't taking place at the tables, though. Of course there was pony racing, but the center stage featured Master Micah and Mistress Dionne facing each other, their subs between their legs. She had her money on Micah for lasting the longest. The competitive leer on his face gave him away.

"So how did you get into all of this, anyway?" Chase asked as they peeked inside the circus cars, where people painted like animals prowled behind cages. "I mean, you were always edgy, but not like this." He waved his hand, encompassing the playroom.

She took the hands and tugged him along. "Let's go somewhere a little more private."

In the center ring the acrobats were performing moves from the Kama Sutra, and in the side rings people were lining up for high-wire sex and trapeze shenanigans. No one would be paying attention to what was going on in the stands, so she led Chase to a darkened corner on the top row of the stadium seats.

"It's like making out in the movie theater," he said.

"But more comfortable." Colleen lifted the armrests to

give them more room. "Now if you want the story, then you're going to have to earn it. Slide down your pants."

Chase looked left and right, confirming that they were alone, then did as he was told. She detached the crotch of her hot pants with a quick tear.

"Never wear anything but those ever again," Chase panted.

Kneeling next to him, she said, "Play with my pussy while I suck you until you're hard. Then I'll start the story."

Not giving him a choice, Colleen sucked on the head while she stroked him. She lavished wide tongue licks over the tip and engulfed his whole cock when Chase started fingering her. The noise of the dungeon's pleasures added to the excitement, and she almost lost herself in the heady sensations of his big fingers stroking her and the slick, sweet hardness in her mouth.

Chase's moans were loud in her ears when she forced herself to stop. "Keep going," she ordered him, too close to deny herself the fast release.

"You are so beautiful when you come," he said, rubbing her.

Shimmying her hips, she reached a dizzying orgasm and disengaged from his fingers. Shaking, she planted herself across his legs and sat on his cock. She threw her head back as her pussy clutched his instinctively.

Chase gritted his teeth. "Don't move or it's all over."

Colleen sat there, reveling in how deep and thick he was. "Now, I'll tell you about Alfie."

"You're mine now," he panted, thrusting up into her. He held her hips tight on him.

"That's right," she said. "But before that I was his."

"Before that you were mine," he snarled, and bucked again. Colleen held on to his shoulders and enjoyed the ride.

"And then it went to shit."

Chase growled. "I can't argue with that."

She clamped down on him again. His head rocked back. She eased her breasts out of the bustier. "Lick my nipples, slave. One lick only on each."

His eyes on fire, Chase did what she asked, his tongue raspy and wet. Colleen bit back a moan.

"He was a whale—one of the big spenders at the casino," she said

"Like me," Chase grunted.

"Yeah, except he won."

"I'll say he did. Can I lick your nipples some more?"

"Not yet," she said, bouncing on him for a few seconds.

"I can't believe we're fucking in public."

"It's not like we're on center stage. We're almost alone."

Chase gripped her hips. "I can hear people going at it a few rows down."

Moving slowly up and down on him now, she asked, "Does it excite you?"

"Hell yeah."

"Good. Now listen to the story. A few days after you and I broke up, Alfie won huge. We had spent some time together. He made me laugh and he was a gentlemen. Which was rare. Too many of those hotshots think they have carte blanche with any casino worker. For the most part, they're right. But Alfie wasn't like that. Anyway, I was still pissed at you and he noticed. He asked me what was wrong. I told him I had broken up with my boyfriend."

"Technically, we weren't broken up."

"Didn't you get my lipstick note?" Colleen pressed her breasts into his face, but moved back when his mouth tried to catch her nipple. "No," she ordered.

"I figured you were mad."

"I slapped you across the face and dumped your luggage into the pool."

"I thought we'd have another chance."

"We didn't," Colleen said, bouncing on him angrily now. She gripped his hair. "Don't you dare come." She fucked him like that, using him to get off, until he was breathing through his teeth,.

She came with a cry, shuddering against him.

"Please," he gritted out.

Getting off him, Colleen got on all fours. "Like this," she said over her shoulder. "Until your knee starts to hurt."

"What knee?" he panted, and crashed into her.

Colleen arched up to meet him as he fucked her hard and fast. The friction was good, and she felt herself building up again. She struggled to get her breath. "So Alfie asked me if I wanted the best orgasm of my life." Colleen paused in the story when Chase growled and thrust deep, then held himself still. "I said hell yes. He made me a deal. If I agreed it was the best I'd ever had, I would marry him. If it wasn't, then he'd give me anything I wanted to make up for it. So I agreed. I figured he'd lick my pussy or fuck me and I'd get a car out of it."

Chase grunted. "I would have bought you a car if you'd asked me."

"Not the point," Colleen panted as he pulled almost completely out before ramming back into her. God, he was amazing. Hard, thick, relentless, and too caught up in her story to remember he was about to come. He stopped again, buried deep.

Colleen wiggled against him, but then remembered she had a story to finish. "Alfie brought me to a BDSM club that I had never heard of. Bought me a Gaultier dress covered in Swarovski crystals, with a matching leash and collar. I was to walk around with him and follow all his orders. I was game."

The memory came flooding back to her. The carpet had been as soft as cashmere where she knelt. He had asked permission to fondle her breasts while she watched the other subs and Doms play. Then he asked to put clips on them. Then to place a vibrator that her underwear would hold in place. She got lost in those sensations until Chase's pounding cleared them. Suddenly that memory was a wisp and it was her own dungeon's floor she was on.

"Come in me," she ordered, and held on for dear life when he let loose. There were no more ghosts between them. Just the slap of their bodies and her moans that she didn't bother to hide. Her place. Her dungeon. Her man. "Fuck me, my love," she whispered.

He drilled her deep and exploded with a ragged cry. Chase rocked into her a few more times, and she leaned down on her elbows to enjoy him. Her orgasm was quieter, but powerful enough that it took her breath.

"Yes," Chase breathed out, pulling out. "Ow, my knee." He sank back on his butt.

"I told you to stop when it hurt."

"It just started to hurt. Besides, I'd walk with a permanent limp for that."

They fixed their clothing and walked back to the rings with their arms around each other. "So that's where it all began?" Chase asked.

"Yeah, I was his sub for most of our marriage, but in the last year before his death he switched it up. I never went back to being a submissive. I like the dominant role too much."

He rubbed her back.

"That's not a deal breaker for you, is it?"

"Colleen, you make me feel like I can fly. You can get me hard with a look. I'm ready to fuck you again, and I can't feel my legs. Nothing is a deal breaker for me."

"Chase, this intensity can't last. You know that, right?"

"Talk to me again when it fades, because right now I want to have a beer and have you sit on my lap."

Colleen hugged him tight. "Get your second wind. Because after that beer, I want to ride your face until I come."

When her phone rang, Colleen almost ignored it, but she saw it was Anya.

"Have a couple of beers. I'll be right back." She gave him a quick kiss and ducked outside the casino playground to take the call.

"How's Paris?"

Chase had followed her out of the dungeon. Maybe she should have made that more of an order, but she changed her mind when he wrapped his arms around her and started kissing her neck.

"Colleen, we don't have the clothes." Anya's anguished cry cut through Colleen's mellow happiness.

For a moment Colleen tried to misunderstand. Maybe Anya meant *she* had no clothes.

"Did you hear me? Fierocity isn't with me."

So much for suspension of disbelief. "What? Did the airline lose it? I'll have their heads."

Chase stepped back, frowning. "Holy shit," he said.

"No, we got the wrong boxes. We have Max's samples."

"How the fuck did that happen?" Colleen shouted.

"How the fuck do I know?" Anya shouted back.

"Okay. No problem." Colleen paced the corridor. "I'll handle this. When do you have to be in Calais?"

"Tomorrow at ten."

Colleen did mental calculations with timelines and couriers and prices. "Go to the location. I'll get you the correct boxes."

"You don't even know where they are," Anya lamented.

"I'll find them. I'll call you when they're in the air."

Colleen hung up and turned to Chase. "Shit. I need to fix this." She dialed Nefertiti, praying she was still at her desk.

"I heard," Chase said, taking off his mask and stuffing it in his back pocket. "I saw Max and Mallory at Cielie's about an hour ago. I'll run up and see if I can catch him."

"Bless you," she said to him. And when Tee picked up, "Holy shit, we're fucked" was what Colleen said to her by way of greeting.

Luckily, Max and Mallory were lingering over their Guinnesses when Chase came charging in. He explained the situation, and they all took off to the lending closet, where Max's designs should have been stored.

Nefertiti was already there, with Colleen and Istvahn. There were boxes all over the floor. Max and Mallory started pawing through the ones closest to the door. Chase pushed through toward Colleen.

"I don't know how this could have happened," Nefertiti said, her voice shrill and panicked.

"No one is blaming you, Tee," Colleen said. "Why don't you check and make sure that the plane is fueled up and ready to fly?"

"It's still at Charles de Gaulle airport." Nefertiti pointed to boxes above her reach. Istvahn grabbed them and tossed them down to Chase.

"What?" Colleen whispered.

"There was no reason to bring it all the way back home and send it out again, duh," Mallory said, but then sobered up when she realized Colleen was stricken.

"Max, over here," Chase said. "These taped boxes have your logo on them."

Max got busy opening them up. "These shouldn't be sealed."

"Don't worry," Nefertiti said, talking over Max's mutterings. "I called in a few favors. You're using Samuel Kincaide's private jet."

"Sam?" Colleen tapped her finger to her lips.

"Who the hell is that?" Chase frowned at Colleen's blush.

"An old friend. He's a financial analyst on Wall Street."

"Actually," Nefertiti said, "he's heading up the M&A department at Shelby Davis Associates."

"No shit." Colleen made an impressed face.

"What the hell is that?" Chase glared at Colleen.

"Mergers and acquisitions at an investment firm with notoriously deep pockets," Colleen explained. And then she gasped when she recognized the pink suit in the box Max had just opened.

"I didn't put your stuff in my boxes," Max said. He held up the Hello Kitty pink suit with black rhinestone skulls. It was her signature piece for the line.

"I know," Colleen said. "What a nightmare. Let's get all these boxes open so we can take inventory."

Mallory took charge. Istvahn made sure Nefertiti was comfortable and not agitating herself too much while she negotiated a last-minute flight plan from JFK to CDG. In the end, they were able to get LaGuardia to Lesquin airport with a few stops in between, and that was even better. It was tight, but the clothes should make it in time for the shoot in Calais.

"How did this happen?" Mallory said. "Is someone trying to sabotage you?"

"I can't think about that right now," Colleen said. "It's probably just a simple error."

"I hope it wasn't my pregnancy brain," Nefertiti moaned. "Maybe I made the mistake?"

"I said it doesn't matter." Colleen went over to hug her. "Your health and the baby's are more important. We're all human and we all make mistakes. We're fixing this. Just get papers ready for Clint to do the clothing exchange."

"Clint?" Max said. "I figured I would go and get them."

"Let Clint go," Colleen said. "Anya will be thrilled, and he'll help keep her calm. He knows the line well enough to make sure he gets everything right, doesn't he?"

"Sure," Max said. "That works for me."

Mallory gripped his hand. "Good, because if you went to Paris without me, I'd be pretty pissed."

"First of all, he's going directly to Lille. Anya went via Paris because it's physically impossible for her to be in France without shopping on the Champs-Élysées. Nord Pas-de-Calais is lovely, though. You could have gone with him."

"I've got double shifts tomorrow. And since I'm not the boss, I can't make my own hours."

Colleen stuck her tongue out at her sister.

"Which is my cue to leave. You're all set. Those five boxes were the entire Fierocity line," Mallory said with a wave.

"I'll put them in the car if you'll stay with Tee," Istvahn volunteered.

"Of course," Colleen murmured.

"I don't need a goddamned babysitter. I'm pregnant, not an invalid."

"He just worries about you." Colleen sat next to her and put an arm around her.

"I know. I'm sorry," Nefertiti sniffed.

"Don't cry," Istvahn said. "It is nothing. I'll be right back."

Chase picked up a box when Nefertiti started weeping, and carried it out of the closet to where a trolley cart was waiting. "Don't worry, man. My sister was the same way when she was having my nephew."

"Thanks," Istvahn said as they loaded up. "And for helping."

"Don't mention it." He walked with Istvahn out to the main entrance, where the truck and Clint were already waiting.

"Are you going to be able to manage all by yourself?" Chase asked as the three of them loaded up the boxes.

"The hard part will be after I land, but Nefertiti is clearing the way for me and hopefully customs will go smoothly and I can pick up a decent truck. Anya's going to meet me at the airport in Lille."

"Good luck." He shook hands with Clint and watched as they pulled out of Couture.

"So Istvahn," Chase said, trying to be casual, "what can you tell me about this old friend Samuel Kincaide?"

"He and Colleen dated for a while, but they're too much alike and it didn't last. They're still friendly."

"How friendly?" Chase scowled. "Is he . . . you know . . . in the lifestyle?"

Istvahn shook his head. "He was never allowed into the club levels."

"Good." Chase wasn't sure why that pleased him, but the relief in his gut was a welcome feeling.

Istvahn's phone buzzed. He read the text and then said, "Colleen brought Tee up to her room. I'm going to check in on them. Colleen said for you to go back to the dungeon and she'll meet you there."

"Okay." Chase shrugged. It wasn't any fun without her. Well, that wasn't completely true. He'd just rather have his hands around his woman than watch everyone else fucking their brains out. Still, she was the Mistress, so what she said went. Once he was in the elevator going down, he wished she'd told him to meet her in the penthouse. Or, even better, back at his place. Wait, his place was a mess. Better off if they stayed here.

CHAPTER 14

The staff development party was still in full swing and getting rowdy. Chase ordered a shot and a beer, and it eased the hard edges off. The Fierocity mix-up could have been a real nightmare. Chase was glad there had been a simple solution. He slammed a second shot, and the tension just rolled right out of him. As he nursed the second beer, he put his back to the bar and did some people-watching. He was itching to try his hand at blackjack, but he was pretty sure Colleen would take a piece off his ass if he sat across from Angie.

A crowd had gathered around a rather unique roulette wheel. Instead of being attached to the table, the giant wheel was attached to a frame. Chase recognized Jana strapped to it and being spun ankle over head. Dante was blindfolded, and of course Jana was completely naked. The wheel had black and red numbers around the outside. In the space between her spread legs were the green zero and double zero.

Chase didn't think it looked too safe and tensed each time Dante let fly. But six spins later, he was elbowing his way up to place a bet on red nineteen. The chips had Colleen's face on them, which he thought was a trip. He quickly lost his stash and was considering what he was willing to do from the job board for another handful. Reading down the list, he discovered that blow jobs were worth ten chips and anal was worth one hundred.

"Something in the middle," he murmured, "and then only if it's Colleen." He nursed his beer and was trying to barter either a hot oil massage or a foot rub for twenty more chips when Dante tapped him on the shoulder.

"Jana needs a break. Get on the wheel."

"I beg your pardon?" Chase said.

"Dom." Dante pointed to himself. "Sub." He pointed to Chase. "Wheel now, or I'll show you what it means to beg."

If he told Dante to go fuck himself sideways with a pitchfork, would that get Colleen in trouble? Probably not; she owned the place. As he opened his mouth, Chase wondered if mouthing off to Dante would get him punished. He didn't want any more abstinence. And if it was just a matter of going for a ride on the wheel a few times, it wasn't worth not seeing Colleen.

He tanked his beer. "You're the boss." He shrugged.

Chase kind of liked the catcalls and appreciated the light slaps on his ass. In a way, it was like he had just sacked the quarterback again. Smiling, he waved to the crowd. Jana helped buckle him in.

"Don't worry," she said. "Master Dante seldom misses."

"Seldom?" Chase wasn't sure seldom was a wide enough margin and had a second to realize he was an idiot before Jana heaved the wheel and it spun around three times before she jumped clear. He heard the thunk as the knife sank in.

"Black twenty-two."

Aside from a slight dizziness, this wasn't so bad. The second turn was uneventful: "Red twelve." That was closer to his face than he liked but still far enough away that

Chase only blinked at the knife. The next spin came up green zero.

"Hey now," Chase said and tried to rip himself down.

Jana tugged the blade out from under his balls. "Don't be such a crybaby," she said.

The wheel spun again before he could retort that when she had a scrotum she could tell him not to bitch, but until then she could jiggle her ass over to the stage and tell Dante to lay off the bladed weapons.

Suddenly, sharp pain pierced his arm. "Fuck," Chase snarled, looking at the hole in his shirt. Dante had only nicked him, but fury took over. "Get me out of this thing."

Jana hurried back over and started unbuckling his legs. "You're all right. It's just a scratch."

"This idiot has no business throwing knives if he can't hit what he's aiming at."

A collective gasp sounded from the watchers.

"Leo, bring me my cat," Dante said with undisguised glee.

Chase wasn't sure why he was calling for pussy at a time like this, but he was glad his legs were free. By the time Jana had taken off the cuffs, the little cut had clotted up. Chase was still pissed, especially when a naked man wearing a penis cage—Chase did a double take. *A penis cage?*—handed Dante a cat-o'-nine-tails.

"Kneel before me, sub, and take your punishment." Dante sauntered over to him.

"Eat shit," Chase said, and hauled off and hit him in the jaw.

Staggering back, Dante struck out with the whip. It hit Chase low on his leg, and the sting spiked his temper. Launching himself at Dante, Chase caught him around the waist and slammed him into the floor. Dante bounced almost as good as a rookie quarterback. Chase was feeling a little too pleased with himself and wasn't paying attention, because he got kneed in the head as soon as Dante recovered. He tackled him back down again. Dante bucked and tried to flip them, but Chase outweighed the bastard by a good seventy pounds.

A whip crack thundered an inch over his head, and Chase instinctively ducked. Dante threw him off but stayed on the floor when Colleen snapped a short whip next to where he was sitting. Dante held up his arms in surrender.

"What the hell is going on here?" She stood over them like a leather-clad avenging angel. The whip dangled in her hand. Chase swore it was almost vibrating with a life of its own.

"Your sub attacked me." Dante eased up into a sitting position. "I demand the right to punish him."

"This maniac stabbed me in the arm." Chase showed her the cut on his biceps.

"In my office, now. And not another word out of either of you."

"Yes, Mistress," Chase said, getting to his feet.

"As my Mistress commands." Dante gave her an artful bow as he rose.

Show-off.

How could he do this to me? Colleen seethed. Both of them. She had to get a grip on her temper before they made it back to her office; otherwise, it could get out of hand very quickly. The elevator ride up was silent except for their breathing. She was pretty sure steam was coming out of Dante's ears.

Colleen waved them into her office. Like she really needed this shit after the Fierocity fiasco and having to calm Nefertiti down. "Sit down," she ordered, slamming her door. She came around the desk. "You boys want to tell me why I saw my sub and one of my Doms fighting like schoolkids?"

They both started talking at once.

"Silence," she snarled out. "Dante, your side of the story first."

"He attacked me."

Colleen waited, holding up a hand to stop Chase's rebuttal. "Is that all you're going to say?"

"He struck me in the face and then tackled me to the ground. I demand—"

"Shut up," she said, cutting him off. She turned to Chase. "Your side."

Please have a good excuse.

"He cut me with one of his knives."

"What?" She wheeled on Dante.

Dante crossed his arms over his chest and looked away from Colleen's glare. "I missed. He was on the wheel and was moving around and the knife pierced his skin."

"Let me see the wound."

"That's not the point," Chase said, pointing to the hole in his shirt.

Colleen ripped the sleeve open to take a look. "It's just a scratch. What were you doing up on the roulette wheel anyway?"

"He ordered me," Chase said. "Said he'd punish me if I didn't go."

"Where the hell do you get off threatening my sub?" Colleen whirled on Dante again.

"He didn't safeword. I thought it was fine."

Colleen arched an eyebrow at Dante, who dropped his gaze. "I didn't miss on purpose," he said. "Which is what he accused me of, and then he embarrassed me in front of the entire club."

"He was going to hit me with a whip. So I punched him," Chase said.

Colleen walked back around her desk and sat down. She practiced her breathing exercises and waited for serenity to flood through her. When that didn't happen, she folded her hands in front of her on the desk. "I can't have fistfights breaking out in my dungeon. You're both lucky this was done on a staff development night and not in Club Inferno. Although the subs are going to talk."

"They'd better not," Dante said darkly.

"Chase," Colleen sighed. "You disrespected a Dom and physically attacked him. If we were in a regular club, the police would have been called and Dante would be well within his rights to press charges."

"He threw a knife at me," Chase protested, gripping the chair's arms until Colleen thought they would crack.

"Which brings me to my next point. Dante, in threatening a sub to make him obey you, you disregarded every rule we have. You have to earn a sub's respect. You may be a Dom, but you are not *his* Dom, and he has no obligation to follow any of your orders."

"I already explained to you—"

"Shut up," Colleen ordered.

Dante sulked in his chair.

"You're both punished. One week of abstinence for Chase and a one-week ban on Club Inferno for you, Dante."

"That's bullshit." Chase bolted to his feet, and his chair went flying.

"I do not deserve a ban," Dante said calmly. "And my reputation was tarnished by his disrespect. I respectfully request the right for me to punish him."

"Come at me, bro," Chase said, waving him on.

"Denied," Colleen spat.

"I'm out of here." Chase slammed the door on his way out.

Dante stayed and waited a few breaths. "That's some sub you've got there."

"You are out of line. You were out of line down there, too."

He stood up and stretched, rubbing his jaw. "You should

have Istvahn watch out for him. He's a beast and can't be controlled."

"I control him just fine." Colleen got up, ready to bodily throw him out of her office.

"I wish you'd reconsider my offer. We understand each other. We want the same things. Chase Fairwood will never fit in here. He's already making things worse by distracting you and your staff. He's a loose cannon."

"I can handle him." She hated that there was enough truth in Dante's logic to make her stomach turn.

"I just don't want to see you hurt."

"I appreciate your concern." She guided him out with a firm hand on his back. "But I've got this. And if I get even a hint that you're forcing subs that aren't yours to obey you again, you'll be out of here so fast you won't know what hit you. Understand?"

"I do." He bowed again. "I apologize for not handling the situation better."

Well, at least one of them apologized.

She nodded.

"If you need me, call." Dante kissed his fingers at her and walked out.

CHAPTER 15

C olleen was still in bed when her phone rang at 11:00 a.m., like it had rung every day for the past week at this time. Against her better judgment, she answered it.

"Technically, I shouldn't be talking to you until tomorrow," she said as a greeting.

"I miss you," Chase said.

"Gotten over your tantrum?" Colleen stared at the ceiling, wishing she could see his face.

"About five minutes after I left. I headed down to New Jersey and took a room there to get some space. I figured if I couldn't have you, I could at least do some heavy betting in Atlantic City and then mooch off my old teammates for a free ticket to yesterday's game."

"Did they win?" Colleen smiled and pulled the comforter over her as she turned on her side to lay her phone on the pillow next to her. He had left sweet voice mail messages every day, but there were also a few drunk texts. She saved them.

SRY 4 BING AN ASSHOLE
I LOVE U SEXEEE BITCCCH

WISH I WAS INSIDE U NOW

FUCK DANTE

"We won. Well, the team won. I just sat on the sidelines and suggested a few plays."

He sounded proud and happy, maybe just a little bit tired.

"So do you think coaching is in your future?"

"Nah. I mean, maybe. I wouldn't turn it down. But I don't think an offer will be coming my way."

"I'd miss you if you were on the road again," Colleen admitted.

"So has my punishment been as hard on you as it's been on me?"

Stretching, she wriggled her toes as the heat in his voice warmed more than just her heart. "Let's just say I'm going to have you all to myself tomorrow night."

"I'm on my way home now. If you want to sneak out tonight, Dante will never have to know."

"I don't give a shit about what Dante knows or doesn't. You didn't have to leave town. When I laid down the law and said a week of abstinence as a punishment, this time I really only meant penetration."

"Now you tell me."

Colleen sat up. "Wait a minute. You stormed out in a fit. You didn't give me a chance to explain."

"I called every day since. This was the first day you picked up."

"Call it a lesson learned then, Chase. I would have given you amazing phone sex." Her bed was beseeching her to lie back down, so she did. It had been a long week.

Dante's suspension had been rough on everyone. His subs Jana and Leo stayed away, too, out of solidarity. She'd even gotten into a fight with Jana over Dante's punishment. After she'd told the little bitch to mind her own business, Jana had given her the silent treatment, which was awkward because she was filling in for Nefertiti.

And because Dante still taught a dance and gymnastics class on the Couture side, Colleen hadn't managed to avoid him altogether, either. Dealing with his martyred looks hadn't been pleasant. With Clint in France and Max fretting about his sportswear, she and the other Masters and Mistresses had been taking up the slack. Colleen rotated her wrist. She was going to get carpal tunnel from all the spanking she'd been doing.

"I needed some time." Chase's sigh was loud through the phone's speakers. "Not from you. To keep from punching his lights out again. Thanks again for not taking any of his shit."

"He was out of line," Colleen said. "First of all, he had no business calling you up onstage. He knew you and I were exclusive. But I also should have told you that while you had to show respect for the other Doms, you didn't have to obey them, either. I assumed that they wouldn't bother approaching you because you were mine. Apparently I underestimated Dante's ego."

"Please tell me you never fucked him."

Colleen rolled over. "I beat him with a whip."

"Did it hurt?" Chase said.

"It didn't hurt me. But he staggered away with a few bruises."

"Good. He's an assclown."

"You're not his favorite person, either." As much as Colleen wanted to lounge in bed all day, she really should get down to her office. Anya would be checking in. She had managed to get a few more French venues to show off Fierocity, and the buzz overseas was making up for the flat line in the States.

"So can I make you dinner at my place tonight?"

"As long as it's a late supper. I need to observe the Hot Spot for a few hours tonight. Does eleven work for you?"

"Are you staying over?" he crooned.

"It depends on whether you piss me off or not."

"There might be roses and candlelight waiting for you."

Colleen considered it. "Why don't you swing by that sex toy shop and pick up a few things?"

"I can do that."

Well, that's a different answer than last time. The punishment had been good for him. She could see an improvement in how he was dealing with things. Now, if it could only stop him from raging first and asking questions later.

"I wish you were here in my bed right now," she told him.

Chase laughed. She heard the engine of his car rev. "I'm still a state away. Maybe I could meet you up at the Hot Spot?"

"Nope," Colleen said. "Your punishment ends at midnight, not a minute before."

After hanging up with Chase, she took a shower and got ready for work. Nefertiti was half asleep at her desk.

"Why don't you go to bed? Or at least catch a nap on the couch in my office."

She wrinkled her nose. "Did you change the sheets?"

"Personally, no. But the cleaning staff would have." Colleen poured Nefertiti a mug of steaming herbal tea. "Drink this."

"I want coffee."

"Any day now," Colleen said cheerfully.

"I hope it's today." Nefertiti stuck out her feet. "I feel like a giant water balloon." She got up. "I think I'm going to take you up on your offer. I'm not feeling so well. And don't you dare call Istvahn." She pointed at Colleen.

"I won't." Colleen said. *Call, that is*, she added to herself silently. However, she texted him about the situation.

She spoke to Anya at Tee's desk so as not to disturb Tee's rest on the couch.

"Fan-fucking-tastic," Anya said when Colleen asked her how it went. "Except for one teeny-tiny detail."

"What's that?" Colleen inspected her fingernails. It was time for a manicure. She made a note to book an appointment at the day spa.

"The private plane you sent with Fierocity and Clint?"

"Yeah?"

"Well, I might have decided to join the mile-high club—on the ground," Anya confessed.

"I care why?" Colleen cracked open her second diet cola of the day.

"Because they thought I was you."

Colleen let gravity take her forehead onto the desk. "You're not serious?"

"I'm afraid they got some great shots of Clint's ass and my legs. They're calling them you and Kincaide."

"Didn't I pay for you guys to have sex in a nice hotel room?" Colleen said.

"Hey, I'm really sorry. I'll totally own up to the pictures."

"Never mind," Colleen rubbed her temples. "I'll do damage control. You make sure the scandal doesn't tank Fierocity."

"The French don't care. In fact, I've gotten a couple of interviews out of it. Paris Match, baby. Later, alligator." Anya rang off.

Colleen couldn't find Sam's number in Tee's computer. She wanted to tell him personally rather than have him find out through social media. Colleen knew Tee had just called him the other day about the plane, so the number had to be around here somewhere. She flipped through a Rolodex that was so obsolete it should be in a museum. Opening and closing drawers, she desperately searched for anything that might have his cell phone number. Colleen could call his company, but she was afraid that they wouldn't put her through.

As she was trying to cyberstalk him, a new email came through. It was Anya with a link to the news article that the National News Machine put on their front page: *"It's Billionaire #2 for Blond Widow—Can Kincaide Survive?"*

Sure enough, Clint's mighty fine ass was captured mid plunge. All you could see of Anya was her fire-engine-red Christian Louboutins— Wait a minute. Those were Colleen's shoes.

Colleen fired back an email bitching about that. Then she went to print the picture out for Tee, who would get a kick out of it. But as Colleen reached for the photo paper from the printer, a crumpled paper on the ground caught her attention. It looked like someone had missed tossing it into the trash. The reason it stood out was because it was her own personal stationery.

She didn't recognize the handwriting, but whoever wrote it had signed Colleen's name. It said:

Recycle Max's boxes for the Fierocity line.

Tape them up and put them on the top shelf of the lending closet.

And then below that, she recognized a note from one of her Club Inferno bouncers who did maintenance work on the Couture side: *All set—Axe.*

Grabbing the note, Colleen put on the answering service and peeked into her office. Nefertiti was snoring silently. She texted Istvahn to come watch over her and then went to see if she could find Axe.

Chase's phone rang just as he hit the Connecticut border. He was hoping it was Colleen rethinking having phone sex with him, but when he glanced at the screen he saw it was Kevan.

"Yo," Chase said. "Miss me already?"

"Son, are you sitting down?" Kevan's voice was angry, and Chase could feel a rant coming on from him.

Groaning, he wished he'd never picked up the phone. "Yeah," Chase said when it became obvious that Kevan was waiting for an answer.

"You were such an angel all week."

"Don't start, man. I told you, Colleen and I are going the distance. You better get used to her because she and I are going to be around for a long time."

"Yeah, well someone should have told her that."

"What are you talking about?" Chase wondered if he should pull over and grab some coffee.

"While you were all pure and shit while the rest of us were knee deep in pussy, your bitch was banging some billionaire on his private plane."

Adrenaline seared through Chase. Every bit of lethargy burned off him in a blast of rage. "You're full of shit."

"Pictures don't lie. I just emailed you."

Chase pulled the Mercedes to the side of the road and put on his four-ways. He scrolled to his email and waited the nine years for the picture to download. "That could be anyone." Chase refused to let any doubt color his voice.

"It was on a private jet owned by Samuel Kincaide. The photographers confirmed it was them."

"Where was this photo taken?" Chase adjusted the image. Kincaide was her ex and he had lent her the plane. He could barely see the woman in the picture, but he was almost positive those calves weren't Colleen's. They'd better freaking not be, anyway.

"Northern France."

"Calais?" Chase asked.

"That's it."

Chase closed the photo. "That's not her. Her business partner is in Calais."

"That's not how the press is reporting it."

"The press is full of shit. She's been in Connecticut this whole week."

"How do you know? You were in New Jersey with us."

"This is all a big misunderstanding. Look, why don't you guys drive on up tonight? She's got a killer dance club called the Hot Spot. We could sit around, have a few drinks, and you can see how crazy she is—about me." He'd have to clear it with her and be in non-dungeon wear, but he was confident he could change her mind about the dance club.

"All right, home slice. I'll give you the benefit of the doubt. But are you sure you want to play the fool in front of the rest of the guys?"

"Just come on down. You'll be buying us drinks all night."

"In your dreams," Kevan said.

Chase took one more glance at the photo. The shoes looked like something Colleen would wear. "Fuck it." He dialed Colleen. It went directly to voice mail. "What the fuck is this I hear about you and Kincaide? It's bullshit, right? Call me."

Colleen found Axe watching the Bikram yoga class through the small window in the door.

"Why don't you just go in?" Colleen asked.

"I'm afraid I'll pass out," he said.

"It's not that warm. Are you ogling anyone in particular?"

"What do you know about Christie?" He angled his head toward the instructor, a pretty redhead with a yoga body and a dirty mind.

"She's single. Vanilla. Used to be a model in Milan until she was in a car accident."

"How vanilla?" Axe peeked in again.

"Enough that she won't go to the Hot Spot even on normal nights."

"Always a first time," Axe said with a shrug.

Colleen's phone buzzed.

"Aren't you going to answer that?"

She shook her head. "I'm in a media shit storm. I need your help. Who gave you this note?"

Axe looked down at it. "Jana."

"Really?"

"Yeah. I thought it was a little weird, but what do I know?"

"Thanks," Colleen said. As she walked away she called out over her shoulder, "Christie likes movies. Every time I do a screening, she's the first one through the door."

"Thank you," Axe said.

Colleen tracked down Jana. She was sitting in the back of Dante's dance and gymnastics class with Leo, moping around like someone who'd lost her collar. Not wanting to interrupt Dante's class and draw attention to herself, Colleen just stood in the doorway and glared her death Domme stare until Jana sensed she was being watched.

When Jana glanced up, she flinched when Colleen held up the memo. Leo started to get up with her, but she waved him off.

"Explain," Colleen said.

Jana's eyes filled with tears. "I was mad at you. You had the best man in the world interested in you and you threw him away like garbage."

"What?" For a moment Colleen thought Jana was scolding her about Chase's punishment. Then she realized Jana only could be talking about one man. "Dante? This was because I wouldn't bottom for your Master? Did he order you to do this?"

"No. No. He'd never cross you. He loves you."

Colleen shook her head. "Jana, obsession isn't love."

"Are you going to tell him?"

"No," Colleen said. "You are. But your punishment is to be banned from Club Inferno for a month."

Jana's mouth opened and shut, but no noise came out.

"And whatever else Dante decides. You're lucky I don't press charges. What you did came very close to sabotaging my business. You do it again and I'll make sure you go to jail. You got me on that?"

"It was stupid. I was angry and jealous. But I'd never hurt the club."

"I am the club," Colleen said, and there was something in her tone that had Jana wincing.

"What's going on out here?" Dante stormed out of his classroom and spat in a furious whisper. "Why are you harassing my sub?"

"I'm not, but how does it feel?" Colleen stuffed the paper in Dante's pants. "I'll let her tell you. Email me what punishment you have decided for her in addition to her ban."

"What?" Dante looked taken aback. He wasn't that good an actor, so she was willing to believe that Jana had acted in the heat of the moment, out of spite. "What did you do?" He gripped Jana around her shoulders and shook.

"Not here in full sight of the Couture people. You can take this to your rooms." Colleen glanced around. They were alone in the hallway . . . for now, anyway.

"Get back in class," Dante ordered Jana. "I'll take care of this," he said to Colleen. "It won't happen again."

"For your sake, Dante, it had better not." Colleen turned on her heel and headed toward her office.

She ignored another call and regretted it when she heard the sirens.

CHAPTER 16

"Just keep me posted," Colleen said. "I'll be there later tonight to give you a break."

She tossed her cell phone on her desk and put her face in her hands. Allowing herself one small sob, Colleen immediately sat up and wiped her eyes with the back of her hand. Crying wasn't going to help Tee or the baby. Neither would Googling high blood pressure during the last trimester. Istvahn had taken Nefertiti's blood pressure and called for an ambulance. Mallory met them at the hospital and would stay with them until Nefertiti's ob-gyn or midwife could get there.

What scared Colleen the most was Nefertiti didn't even put up a token resistance. Normally she'd say she was fine and they were fussing for nothing. In fact, Tee was scared, and that brought out all Colleen's protective instincts. Colleen wanted nothing more than to follow the ambulance, but Istvahn told her to wait. They would be just sitting around and waiting for a few hours, and Colleen would only be in the way until they had found Nefertiti a room and gotten her settled in. Tee was with the doctors right now, and Istvahn would contact her if she was needed.

Colleen agreed, only because she had things to do here first and Istvahn would be able to handle the details for Nefertiti. She toyed with the idea of bringing Dante in to help at the Hot Spot tonight, but after the altercation with Jana today, maybe it was for the best that he stayed away from her. She considered closing the Hot Spot tonight, but she hated disappointing the clients.

They were lining up at the door now. She didn't want a bunch of disgruntled people wandering around. Anyway, she had Micah and Steve, with Max and Dionne on call. They should be all right to keep an eye on anyone who crossed the line. Her bar managers were also the best in the business, so it freed her and the Doms to walk around the club searching for potentials and stopping trouble before it happened.

The first few hours went well. They reached capacity and offered drink vouchers at Cielie's and Shira's with a pager. Colleen was dressed in Gaultier, a corset dress shaped like a butterfly; Dita von Teese had worn the blue-and-black version at the 2014 spring fashion show. Colleen's was red and gold, and she wore the stockings and elbow-length gloves to match.

Someone jostled her from behind, and she nearly sloshed her champagne over the one-of-a-kind dress. Colleen turned to glare at the oaf, and came face-to-face with Kevan Lewis, one of Chase's old teammates.

"What are you doing here?" She used the tone she usually reserved for off-the-rack clothes.

"We came to check out your nightclub."

Colleen looked around and spotted three more players heading toward them. "This is a private club. I'm afraid you have to be invited by a member."

"Chase invited us."

"Did he?" She raised her eyebrow. That was news to her. "He didn't mention it to me."

"You two weren't talking much last week." Kevan ran a hand over his jaw and looked her up and down. "I heard you were very busy with Samuel Kincaide."

"My relationship with Chase is none of your business." She turned to walk away, but he grabbed her upper arm and yanked her back.

She threw her glass at him, which freed her up to toggle her microphone. "Code five mid-bar."

"You little bitch." Kevan wiped away the liquid and dragged her toward his buddies.

Crap. If Istvahn had been here, this never would have happened. She grabbed Kevan's thumb and yanked down hard. Kevan let her go, probably mostly to save himself a hand injury, because his grip had been solid.

"You remember Trent, Dorie, and Jason, right?" Kevan said, flinging her into the center of them.

Where the hell was Micah?

"I haven't had the pleasure." She left the microphone on, so she was still broadcasting to her team. They'd know they'd be facing four rowdy jerks.

"I'd like to give you the pleasure," Trent said. "There's a room over in the corner where you can suck my dick. It's all private-like."

"Go to hell. I thought you were Chase's friends."

"We are, bitch. That's why we came here. You don't get to fuck around on our bud when he's not even flirting with another chick all week." Dorie went to poke her, but she grabbed his finger and twisted. He pulled away and dodged her kick to his knee.

Jason shoved her back into Kevan, who wrapped his arms

194

around her, trapping her arms. Colleen searched over their heads. Still no sign of security.

"Are you assholes looking for a jail sentence? Get out of my club before I have you arrested for assault and harassment."

"We'll press charges right back," Jason snarled.

"For what?" Colleen spat. She stamped down, trying to smash Kevan's foot. Finally she back-kicked into his shin, and he shoved her away.

"Ow, you bitch. For doing things like that," Kevan said.

"You really want to go on record that I beat you up?" Colleen said, blowing back a lock of hair that had fallen into her face from the struggle. Finally she saw Micah and Steve bearing down on the group. Jesus, they were going to have to work on the response time.

"I'll tell you what," Kevan said. "Break up with Chase. For good this time, and it ends here. No publicity, no nothing."

"You're no good for him," Jason added. "He needs a down-home kind of girl. You're not in his class."

"Me, on the other hand," Trent said with a hand on his heart, "I just got a forty-million-dollar four-year contract. You and I could make some hard-core plays. I ain't an old man, but I got the cheddar to keep you in the style that you've grown accustomed to. Just I need a little test drive, if you know what I mean."

"Get these assholes out of here and put a permanent ban on them for here and every one of my hotels worldwide," Colleen said to her two Doms as they arrived on the scene.

"There's four of us and only three of you, and one of you is a woman," Kevan pointed out.

Micah kicked the back of Trent's knee hard enough that he went down. He caught Jason's punch, then spun him around and cuffed him. Steve gut-punched Dorie, shoving him into Kevan hard enough that they both lost their balance. Colleen stepped aside as they crashed to the ground, leaning over to handcuff Dorie while he was dry-heaving. Steve moved around them, light on his feet for a big man. He stomped a boot into Kevan's nose. When Kevan howled and put his hands up to cover the gushing blood, Steve cuffed him as well. Micah finished securing a sobbing Trent, and the four men didn't look so tough now.

"Gentlemen, you are being escorted to the doors of Couture," Colleen said, moving out of the way of the blood splatters from Kevan's bashed-in nose. "If you're not out of here in five minutes, I will call the police and add trespassing to the charges being filed. You're welcome to talk to my lawyers after that." Colleen dusted her hands over the lot of them.

Two other security men rushed in and helped Steve and Micah with removing the trash. She would review the tapes to check the time. It had seemed like a half hour, but in actuality it had probably been less than five minutes. Rubbing her shoulders, Colleen was annoyed to realize she was shaking.

Chase saw his friends as he got out of his car in the parking lot. "Yo," he called.

"Where have you been?" Kevan said, his face half obscured by his balled-up shirt.

"You guys weren't fighting?" Chase groaned.

Trent was limping, Dorie looked like he was going to puke any minute, and Jason was clenching and unclenching his fists.

"That bitch girlfriend of yours had her bouncers beat us up and throw us out." Jason got up into his face.

"What the hell did you guys do?" Chase grabbed Jason by the shirt and twisted.

"Nothing, man. We were having a good time. She got all bent out of shape when we tried to ask her about Kincaide.

That's when she snapped her fingers and ten big guys threw us out. One of them busted Jason's face, and the other one might have put Trent out of the game."

"Oh, man." Chase took a good look at Trent. He wasn't walking well at all.

"One of her thugs ambushed him," Jason said, pulling free from Chase's grip.

"Was it Dante?" Chase asked, thinking it was just like that little creep to sneak up on a guy and sucker-punch him.

"Yeah, I think so," Trent said. "I gotta go and ice this up. Coach will kill me if I can't play on Sunday. Dude, what if I can't play?" Panic tinged his voice, and Chase winced in sympathy.

"Don't worry about it. It was just a bar fight. It'll be sore, but you should be all right in a few days." *I hope.* "Here's the keys to my place." Chase gave them the address for the GPS. "I'll figure out what the hell is going on and meet you guys there later."

"Chase, man," Dorie said, "be careful."

"I don't need to be careful," he said. "I don't want to be careful." After a week of feeling older than dirt and twice as useless, Chase had wanted to see Colleen. He didn't want to fight. He didn't want to beg forgiveness. He wanted to bridge his two worlds together so his football friends could hang out somewhere where he was still relevant.

But that wasn't meant to be because Dante had thought he could take out his aggravation on Chase with his friends. But he'd show him that wasn't going to fly. Chase stormed out of the parking lot and headed to the Hot Spot. Fuck Dante and his bullshit. Dante had gone too far now. He had no right to mess with a man's career. Trent was one of the best tight ends in football. Dante was way out of line with all his Domliness if he thought he could hide behind Colleen

197

this time. In fact, the ball club would probably sue the shit out of Colleen for this. What was she thinking?

He burst into the Hot Spot, bypassing the line of waiting people; Colleen had white-listed him weeks ago. He couldn't see her right away and his gut twisted, wondering if she was sharing a bottle of Johnny Walker Blue with Samuel Kincaide. Was that why she had hustled his friends out so fast? Chase caught sight of her by the stage, where a bunch of naked people were walking down a runway. She looked like a dejected butterfly in a dress more silly than hot.

No one was near her, especially not Dante and not Samuel Kincaide, who was a billionaire and had two good knees—at least until Chase got through with him, if he was sleeping with Colleen. As he approached her, Chase's focus narrowed on her smile. It was plastic. She was performing again. Maybe Kincaide was stalking around here with a net waiting to capture her. Chase came up from behind her, whirling her around.

She drew her fist back. "Chase?" She blinked in disbelief. "What are you doing here?"

"Stop with the punishment shit." He held up his hand. "I want to talk to you."

Her welcoming smile trembled and then dried up to a firm line. A warning bell went off in his head, but he was too pissed off to slow down. "I've been calling you all day."

She closed her eyes. "I know. I'm sorry. It's been crazy." Colleen put her arms around him.

He stiffened. No, she wasn't going to redirect him with sex.

"You're not going to believe what—"

Chase put her at arm's length. "Trent may never play football again."

"W-what?" Colleen stuttered.

"You need to keep your Doms in line like you keep the subs."

"Obviously I'm not doing a bang-up job in that department." She put her hands on her hips.

"I drove six hours to be with you tonight."

"About that," she sighed. "I have to cry off for tonight. There was an—"

"You're not invited anyway. The guys are staying at my place."

"You're letting those jerk-offs stay with you? After what they pulled?" she shouted.

"Those jerks are my friends. They were only trying help in their own fucked-up way, and you threw them out."

Colleen was unable to speak for a moment.

"You're the last person they want to see tonight. Unless you're willing to come without your goons and we can all talk like rational people."

"Rational people?" Colleen glanced down at the glass in her hand, filled with a dark liquid, and then glared at him.

"Don't you fucking dare," Chase warned.

Which was probably like waving a red flag at a bull—or in this case a butterfly. He was too close to dodge as she tossed it in his face. Chase managed to close his eyes in time.

"Rum and coke," he said as the sticky liquid dripped down his face. "Real mature."

"You have no fucking idea what you're talking about. But that's pretty much standard for you, isn't it?" she spat out. "And a six-hour drive? What did you do, go back to Atlantic City after the game?"

"So what if I did?"

"You couldn't have been in much of a rush to see me, then."

"You weren't answering my calls," he shouted at her.

All of a sudden, Max and another Dom he recognized

from the dungeon, but whose name he couldn't remember, showed up at his shoulders.

"Oh, what? Dante couldn't be here this time?" Chase sneered at them. "Are you going to gang up on me and toss me out? You're going to need a few more guys."

Colleen shook her head. "Go home, Chase. You're delusional. And I don't have the energy to sort through this shit tonight. I've got more important things to worry about."

"Is that right? A week apart and I'm not important? You made me wait a whole week just to talk to you, and now you can't spare five minutes? Fuck you." Chase shook off Max's hand.

"Hey, man," Max said. "Calm down."

"Fuck you too, Max."

Chase turned and shoulder-checked the other Dom out of the way.

"I didn't say you weren't important," Colleen said. He heard her sigh. "If you hadn't stormed out of my office, last week would have been much different."

He turned back. "Your power trips are getting out of hand."

"Are they?" she said, all trace of emotion gone. She could freeze ice cubes with her tone.

"Your life is more than the dungeon. You don't always need to be in control."

"Really? Is that so someone like you can call the shots? I've got news for you, Chase." She closed the distance between them.

It pissed him off that Max and the Dom were still flanking her. Did they think she needed a bodyguard? From him? Where was Istvahn, anyway? He was expecting the big Russian to put him in a full nelson and toss him out on his ass any minute now.

"Your tantrums are getting old," she said. "You're worse

than a two-year-old, the way you blow up and rage and then come back like a dopey puppy looking for forgiveness. You owe me respect, and if not that, then at the very least you owe me the benefit of the doubt. But you barrel into my club, get in my face, and start talking about shit you know nothing about? Typical Fairwood."

"You're high maintenance." He pointed at her.

"No shit, Sherlock." She put her hands on her hips. "You knew that going in. What's your excuse for being a prima donna?"

"I can't handle this right now. I'm going back to my friends, who are probably going to press charges against Dante, and the league is going to come after you if Trent can't play."

"Bring it." Colleen gestured come here at him.

"You're a crazy bitch." He twirled his finger beside his temple.

"And you're done. You're the last possum to call me that tonight."

"Possum?" Of all the things she could have called him, that wasn't what he thought was going to top the list. It threw him, the way she said it with such vicious glee.

"Yeah, footballers who play dead at home and get killed on the road."

"Oh," Chase said, a grin tugging at his lips. "You want to play?"

"Get the fuck out." Colleen glared at him.

"Let's go, man," Max said with a friendly hand on his shoulder. The other Dom just glowered at Chase.

"I'll tell you what," Chase said over his shoulder to her. "You're the one that's going to be punished now. Don't bother calling me. I'll call you when I feel you've learned your lesson."

"Chase, for God's sake stop digging," Max whispered in his ear.

Colleen gave him the bird. He blew her a kiss.

It hit him driving home that he never did get her side of the story.

Asshole.

CHAPTER 17

C hase shifted in his booth. He'd already banged his knee against the iron pole twice. Max had called him a few days after his fight with Colleen. They were meeting at a local diner because he was persona non grata at Couture. She'd changed her cell phone number, and his calls didn't even go to her secretary anymore. Some new chick took a message and said she'd pass on the information to Colleen but that Chase shouldn't expect a call back.

He'd fucked up.

Again.

And he had no idea how to make it better.

His friends had drunk all his booze, and in the morning Trent was walking fine and Kevan's nose looked almost normal. Then they'd gone back on the road, leaving Chase alone with his PS3 and his bobble head.

When he agreed to meet Max, Chase had been hoping that he would bring a peace offering from Colleen, but it had been forty-five minutes and an entire stack of pancakes and her name hadn't come up once.

Chase was trying to figure out how to address the elephant in the room when the lion came striding into the diner. Istvahn glanced neither left nor right but walked straight to the booth where they were sitting. Max looked up when Istvahn stopped at their booth.

"Is Tee all right?" Max said. "The baby?"

"Still nothing. She's hooked up to like thirty monitors, so at the slightest hint of a problem they'll induce, but they're still hopeful that they can do it naturally."

Max held out his hand. "Good luck, man."

They shook.

"Care to sit down?"

"No, I have to get back to the hospital. I came to give him something."

Chase tensed. He was at a disadvantage sitting, and the table would make things awkward if the big Russian started something. Istvahn reached inside his jacket. Chase half rose out of the seat, maneuvering to tackle him to the ground if he pulled a gun. But instead Istvahn removed a DVD case with two fingers and tossed it on the table.

"That better not be a sex tape," Chase joked.

"You've got one last chance," Istvahn said.

"Or what? You're going to kill me?" Chase gave a half laugh to ease the tension.

No one laughed. Hell, Istvahn didn't even blink.

"What's the DVD?" Max asked.

"Security tapes. Clint edited them. I feel that Mr. Fairwood needs to see what actually happened that night. The lawyers have the unedited version if he feels the need to verify what he sees."

"He's sitting right here," Chase said, annoyed that Istvahn was talking over his head as if he wasn't even there. "If Colleen wants me to review this, all she had to do was ask.

I'll come back to Couture and review the footage there." He rose, but Istvahn pushed him back down again.

"Colleen does not know I'm here. She would be within her rights to fire me for giving you this."

Chase picked up the DVD. "Wait—why are you giving this to me, then?"

"Colleen has been more than an employer to me and Nefertiti. She's family. I think she can do worlds better than you, Fairwood."

"Like Samuel Kincaide?" Chase sneered.

"Yes."

"So you must be overjoyed, then."

"They're not together."

"I read the papers," Chase said bitterly.

"No, you read the Internet. If you're going to believe everything you read there, you might be interested in the women who had a third breast added to her chest."

"Is she topless?" Chase leered, but then realized neither Max nor Istvahn was smiling.

"I don't know if you and Colleen will last," Istvahn said.

"Thanks a lot."

"But what I do know is that if this doesn't get addressed immediately, you'll never find out. Colleen deserves the closure."

"Nothing is closed between us," Chase said. "We're in a cooling-off period."

"How did that work for you the last time?" Istvahn countered.

"Is she seeing Samuel Kincaide?" All of Chase's nightmares would come true if the next piece of gossip he read was about Colleen's honeymoon with the Wall Street power-house. He was their age. There was no hope of him kicking the bucket anytime soon.

"At three o'clock this afternoon you will be allowed in

Couture. At two fifty-nine or three-oh-one, you will be denied."

Chase flipped the DVD case open. "Does she know I'm coming?"

"No. She wouldn't be available if she knew you were going to be in the building. You've got one chance at this. Don't fuck it up."

"What if she won't see me?"

Istvahn didn't respond. He turned and walked out.

"Can you believe that guy?" Chase thumbed in Istvahn's general direction.

"It's not Kincaide you have to worry about," Max said, staring into his coffee. "You're going to lose her, but it's going to be to someone in the lifestyle."

"Who? Dante?"

"Here, use my laptop to watch the video. I'm going to go get some pie at the counter. I don't want to see it again. I was there. I was too far away to get to her in time."

"What's that mean?" Chase asked.

"We'll talk after you watch it." Max picked up his coffee cup and left.

Chase watched the video four times. The audio had been taken directly from her microphone. The picture quality was grainy, but he could see she was blocked in by four big football players and being tossed around between them.

Those bastards.

He was watching it a fifth time when Max came back and shut his laptop.

"Do you think it's doctored?" Max asked.

It had never crossed Chase's mind that it might be. Chase didn't trust himself to speak. He just shook his head.

"Why are you watching it over and over?"

"Where was Istvahn?" Chase muttered.

"In the hospital. Tee had a scare. Colleen was on her way there when you showed up."

Chase closed his eyes. "She'll never forgive me. Hell, I don't deserve forgiveness."

"Maybe, maybe not. Does that mean you're not going to try?"

Chase rested his elbows on the table and put his forehead in his palms. "She was right. I always do this. I didn't even give her a chance to tell me what happened. I should have been there. I should have protected her. At the very least, I should have listened to her. There is literally nothing I can say to make things right."

"Then don't say anything."

"What?" Chase pulled his head up to look at Max. "I just walk in there and sink to my knees and silently beg for forgiveness?"

"That's a start. I'd put my forehead on her boot if I really was sorry."

"You? You'd put your forehead on her boot?" Chase snorted.

"If I was her sub, yes. If I was in love with her and was about to lose her, yes. I wouldn't say a fucking word until she told me to."

The last person Colleen expected to see walk in her office was Chase Fairwood.

"Jana, what the fuck?"

But there wasn't any answer. Colleen met him halfway, about to toss him out of her office, before he could say one word about his stupid teammates. But before she could order him to get out, he did the strangest thing: he dropped to his knees. Hands clasped behind his back, knees spread, gaze lowered.

Colleen's world tilted a little bit. This was something she never thought she'd see. He even had good form. She crossed her arms, tapped her foot, and waited. He still said nothing. He was wearing one of Max's tracksuits. Had Max set this up? Walking to the door, she peeked out, but no one was there. Colleen closed the door and locked it. She should tell him to get off his knees. He wasn't used to that position, and his knee would lock. But that would mean engaging with him, and right now she wasn't in the mood for a fight.

"Take off your shirt, slave." Maybe if she could piss him off enough he'd leave.

To her surprise, he unzipped the jacket and pulled it and his shirt off. Then he immediately clasped his hands behind his back again.

Sitting back down at her desk, Colleen tried to figure out his angle. "Your clothes offend me," she said with a silent apology to Max.

Chase immediately removed the rest of his clothes, all the while never looking up at her. When he was naked and kneeling before her, Colleen had a hard time remembering she was mad. She still was, but it seemed a shame to waste a perfectly good slave. Then she noticed Chase had pulled out a riding crop. He left it on the floor in front of him. His hands were behind his back.

Swooping it up, she slammed the tip on her desk. Chase never flinched, just continued to stare at the floor.

All right, this is getting freaky. She didn't think Chase had ever been this quiet in her presence unless he was sleeping. Colleen bent the riding crop, hoping to snap it in two. But that didn't work, so she pulled out her trash can and dumped it in there. No spanking. No matter how much she was tempted to cross his back with a cat, she knew his hard limit. She wouldn't violate his trust. Truly, she should have just sent him packing. Hell, she still could. But first she'd make him sweat.

Determined to ignore him, she turned back to her desk

and tried to read her next email. Colleen could still see him out of the corner of her eye, though. Naked and sexy, utterly submissive. This really wasn't fair. And damn it if her panties weren't damp from it.

"I'm livid with you."

He still said nothing, but he lowered his head to the floor, stretching his arms over his head in supplication.

"You never gave me a chance to explain what your asshole friends did in my club."

Chase remained where he was.

"Then you picked a fight with me and tried to insult and embarrass me."

Still no movement.

"And stormed out in a pique, *again*."

She whirled back to her desk and stared at her desk calendar. She must have an appointment she could get to. Hell, she'd make one up. She stood up to leave, but couldn't tear her eyes away from Chase, naked and utterly submissive.

"Come here, slave," she ordered.

Chase crawled to her, which got her going even more. Damn him, anyway. She pulled down her panties. She kicked them into his line of sight and waited to see if he would break character. But he didn't. She sat down on her office chair again. Lifting up her skirt, she hooked one leg over her chair.

"Make me come with just your tongue."

Chase moved in closer and put his face between her thighs. Colleen nearly came off her seat when his stubble brushed against her thighs. She had wanted to go back to work, put the keyboard on his head, and pretend he was a vibrator. But the moment his tongue dipped inside her, all thought fled. Flinging her head back, Colleen grabbed a handful of his hair and held him in place. His tongue probed and licked, alternately laving up and down her slit and then circling her clit. Her body jolted with each touch as if she was connected to an electrical outlet.

Colleen barely recognized the sounds coming out of her mouth. He broke his silence with a long moan of satisfaction when she gasped and shook, drenching his face.

"Thank you," she said, pushing him back with a heeled foot as she dropped it back to the floor. "Wipe your face with my panties. You may keep them for pleasing me."

Colleen turned back to her desk and tried to read the email again. She figured he'd say something or get up and leave. Either way, the seductive spell would be broken. But he didn't move, and she could see that delicious hard cock standing at attention. Plus, she really should give his knee a break.

"Stand, slave," she ordered.

Again Chase did so without a word. His eyes were still downcast. He was hers utterly to command. Damn him. She didn't want to forgive him. Chase had been an inexcusable jerk. He had jumped to conclusions again. He had raged at her again. And he had stormed out on her.

Again.

Colleen glared at him, arguing with him in her head, since he wasn't giving her the satisfaction of a rip-roaring fight. But . . . he was giving her satisfaction.

"Slave, you will pull out the couch into a bed and make it with the clean sheets in the drawers over there. Come back and kneel before me when you're finished."

Still silent, Chase did as he was told. Colleen pursed her lips. There was no way this was going to last, but she was going to enjoy it while it did. These last few days had been hellish. The media was all over her and Sam. He'd called her and they'd laughed about it. Still, the eyewitnesses coming forward with stories of them having sex all over Europe . . . it was almost depressing that it wasn't true. Sam just wanted to ignore it and let it die out. Colleen wanted to rebut every lie. Unfortunately, if you fed the troll, it grew. Sam was right to let it go. Easy for him to say; he was about to go on an extended vacation to Hawaii.

Again, the work email didn't hold her attention, and Colleen found herself watching the flex of muscles on Chase's backside and legs as he worked to set the bed up. When he was kneeling before her again, she said, "Good slave. I am pleased. You get to fuck me. But you aren't to say anything and you are to keep your eyes shut."

If she had to peer into his eyes, this magical fantasy would be over and she didn't want to face reality. "If you please me, I'll give you permission to come. If you don't, you can leave and finish yourself off outside of my presence. Nod once if you understand."

Chase nodded.

"Good. Lay on your back and keep your eyes closed. Don't make me blindfold and gag you. At the first flutter of your eyelids or at the first word you utter, I will. Understand?"

He nodded again.

"Go," she ordered.

Her heart was beating out of her chest and she couldn't remember the last time she'd been this excited. She was shaking. Chase followed her instructions to the letter, folding his arms behind his head. This gave her a spectacular view of his biceps and abs, and of course his cock. It was still hard, and her fingers itched to touch him.

She changed out of her business suit and considered getting dressed up in bondage wear, but in the end Colleen decided this had to be simple. Flesh on flesh, naked and genuine. Without preamble, she climbed on the bed and then sat astride him, guiding that thick, hard, cock home.

"Oh," Chase shouted, not prepared for her actions.

She didn't put a gag on him for it. She liked the sound almost as much she liked him full and deep inside her. Yes. Colleen rose until he was almost falling out of her, and then she slowly lowered herself back down. She did it again, feeling the sweet glide of his body moving through hers, and again. Chase gripped the bedsheet, and his face was an expression of sheer pleasure. Colleen took him slow until his hips started to twitch. She then bounced hard and he grunted, biting his lip. His nostrils flared and his back arched. Riding him faster, she leaned over so her breasts rubbed up against his chest. Her hair brushed his face and she could feel his breathing speeding up. She stopped and went back to the slow ride, except this time she let him slip out.

"Oh," he groaned again, lifting his hips up as if he was still fucking her.

Colleen straddled his head. "You know what I want now, don't you?" She brushed her pussy against his lips.

He nodded.

She sank down and moved until they were both comfortable, and then she rubbed her pussy against his mouth. His tongue fucked her, when she was still enough for it. But mostly she was out of patience and used it to bring herself to another spectacular orgasm.

"I love your tongue," she moaned as it shook through her.

His answering groan was full of satisfaction and his smug smile was the first hint of the old Chase. She missed him. Crap. She hadn't wanted to. She stroked him, happy to have the familiar thick weight to play with. Colleen rubbed him like she had fucked him, slow and long, and then fast hard strokes. Throwing his arm over his eyes, Chase trembled as he gave himself over to her.

Finally.

"You're mine to play with as I will," she told him.

He nodded.

"I control your orgasms."

He nodded.

"Open your eyes."

There he was. She read heat, longing, and a fever of passion in his eyes. And love. So much love, Colleen nearly cried.

"You may speak," she said.

"I love you."

Colleen waited for the caveat, but when none came, the need that rushed through her defied all reason, all rational thought. She lunged for his mouth and kissed him reverently.

"So . . . sorry. Please . . . forgive me," Chase muttered between kisses. "Love you . . . so much."

"Fuck me," Colleen whispered. "Take me. Now."

They were still kissing when he thrust into her. Their legs entwined and their lovemaking became slow and unrushed.

"You can come," she murmured in his ear.

"You first, my sweet Mistress." Chase rocked into her in a punishing rhythm that she matched gladly.

The world narrowed down to just the two of them, this bed, and the slap of their flesh joining. Colleen wrapped her arms around his neck and refused to stop kissing him, even as she shrieked her release against his mouth.

"Yes," he crooned. "I love it when you come on my cock. Or my tongue. Hell, I love it when you come."

"Chase," she cried, still shuddering from the aftershocks. Each nerve ending was on fire. Colleen shook and gasped, but Chase didn't stop. "Please," she begged.

"One more," he grunted, and pulled out.

He flipped her over on all fours and thrust back in her before she had the thought to complain. All finesse was gone. He pounded into her.

"Yes. Yes. Yes." Each cry was a little louder until she came screaming his name. "Chase."

He yelled back, "Mine." Coming hard, Chase continued the hard slaps of their bodies until she thought she would pass out from pleasure. He pulled out and collapsed next to her. She crawled on top of him and sprawled over his body, satiated.

"Now that's what I call an apology," she said.

He stroked her back. "Can we end all our fights like this?"

"As long as you don't pick fights just so we can screw around during the workday."

He hugged her tight. "Please don't ever give up on me. I know I'm an asshole. I'm working on it."

"The next time you storm out of here in a fit of anger, either you come back like you just did or don't come back at all." Colleen had to draw the hard line. If she had to put up with his childish outbursts, then she would make sure she enjoyed his apologies.

"I will always come back," he promised. "No one can compare to you."

She believed him. He never strayed, never cheated. She could put up with anything as long as he was true to her. "I love you, Chase." Colleen hugged him tight. "Even if you are an asshole sometimes."

"Thank you." His lips quirked up in a small smile.

She nuzzled against his neck as he petted and caressed her. Colleen liked hearing his heartbeat come down from racing to normal. He would never be a true submissive. If she really needed the sexual power a thrall gave her, she'd never get that from Chase. She played with his chest hair as he rubbed her back. But she had plenty of clients that fed her Domme side without sex, so maybe Chase could feed the sexual side, and together she'd be satisfied.

The alternative was falling in love with a true submissive

male, and that would be impossible while her heart and body still clamored for Chase's. The slight snore woke her and she wasn't sure if it was him or her. Then her phone notified her of an incoming text.

It was Istvahn.

911.

CHAPTER 18

"Can't you drive this thing any faster?" Colleen held on to the door as Chase illegally passed someone on the right.

"It's a Mercedes, not a Bugatti," he told her, grinning. "We'll get you to the hospital in time. It's not like you're the one about to give birth."

She pressed the heel of her hand into her aching gut. "Tell that to my stomach."

"Is there something I should know?" Chase slid a sidelong glance at her. "I didn't wear protection."

"I'm on the pill, you ass."

"Oh."

Did she imagine the dejected note in his voice?

He took the hospital exit at warp speed and had to jam on his brakes as three lanes merged into one at the stoplight.

"Damn it." Colleen tried to open the door, but the safety locks were in place. "Let me out here."

"What are you doing? Are you trying to get yourself killed? Nefertiti is in the hospital surrounded by doctors and nurses in the finest birthing facility in the country. Istvahn is there. You're not needed. She's got this covered on her own."

Colleen recoiled as if slapped.

Chase grabbed her hand. "Honey, she's going to be fine."

"She's asking for me. What if she thinks I forgot about her?"

"Don't be ridiculous."

"What if she's scared?"

"Istvahn is there. He's the father."

Colleen sniffed. "I told her I'd be in the birthing room with her. She wanted me, not him."

"Sometimes life has other plans."

They got through the red light, and Chase pulled up to the entrance so she could go in while he parked. Istvahn had told her the floor but not the room. He wasn't answering any of the texts she was sending. Colleen pressed the elevator button several times, but that didn't make it go faster. She burst into the floor, sparing a glance at the lounge. Istvahn wasn't there. The nurses at the center station glanced up when she stalked over.

"I'm here to see Nefertiti Desmond. I'm her birthing coach."

The two women exchanged a glance.

Fear took the strength out of Colleen's knees. She knew she should have insisted on a private hospital with an on-call doctor.

"Better late than never," a sleepy voice said from behind her.

Whirling, Colleen saw Tee lying back on a wheeled bed with an adorable little bundle in her arms. Istvahn strode beside the bed, fingers twitching and his gaze going everywhere as if searching out threats. His fingers clenched and patted his jacket. Was he looking for his Glock?

"This is our daughter, Ezina," Nefertiti said, shifting so Colleen could get a peek at the beautiful, tiny face.

Ezina gave a big yawn and blinked up at them.

Colleen fell in love.

"Ezina, this is your godmother. She's fashionably late."

Sniffing back tears of happiness, Colleen said, "No, Ezina was early. A terrible faux pas, but we'll forgive her just this once. She's new at this."

"Can Colleen and I have a few minutes alone?" Nefertiti said to Istvahn once she and the baby were back in the room.

Istvahn glanced around the room again for threats and gave a curt nod.

"I'm so sorry I'm late." Colleen gripped Nefertiti's hand.

"Don't worry about it. Istvahn stepped up. He did pretty good, although I thought he was going to faint dead on the floor when Ezina came out."

"She's beautiful." Colleen ran her finger over the baby's downy head.

"How are things at Couture?"

Tucking the blanket around Tee's feet, Colleen said, "Everything is fine. Everything will be just as we discussed once you come back. We'll have a little crib and a nanny on call. You have nothing to worry about."

Tears filled Nefertiti's eyes. "I know this is the post-pregnancy hormones talking, but I'm not sure I can be a good mother."

"Too late. You already are." Colleen leaned in to kiss her on the cheek. "And I think Istvahn is a great baby daddy."

"Ass." Nefertiti snorted.

The doctor came in and shooed Colleen out.

"Do you need me to get you anything?" Colleen asked.

Nefertiti shook her head sleepily.

Istvahn was guarding the door like the president was inside.

"How are you doing?" Colleen asked when the door shut.

"Fine."

"You want a shot of vodka?"

He slid an amused glance at her. "You got a bottle in your purse?"

"I can get a bottle of Stoli Elit here in about an hour."

"Done."

She rubbed his arm. "When was the last time you slept?"

He blinked. "I dozed in the chair."

"Why don't you go home and . . ."

Istvahn was already shaking his head.

Chase sprinted into the reception area but skidded to a stop when she gave him a thumbs-up.

"Let me know when she's free or if you need anything," Colleen said.

"Will do," Istvahn said.

She walked over to Chase and dragged him away from an adoring fan. "Excuse us, please."

"Everything went all right?" Chase asked.

Linking her arm with his, she guided him out into the hallway. "Yes. Baby Ezina and mom are doing just fine. Istvahn's getting closer to fine, but he's not there yet."

"I owe him." Chase turned her into his arms for a hug. "If he hadn't shown me the club's tapes, who knows when we would have sorted this all out. Maybe never, if Dante had his way."

"Don't blame Dante—at least not completely. He's a manipulator and an opportunist. He saw the rift between us and used it to his advantage."

"Next time he can see my fist again."

Colleen grabbed the fist he was shaking and kissed it. "He's not pressing charges from the last time you punched him. Don't press your luck."

"I can't help it. I have to."

And when he sank down on one knee, her first thought was that he'd better be careful of his injury, followed by a brief disapproval of his form. If he was going to offer submission in a crowded hospital, he should at least do it right. Then that faded and all the air left her lungs when he pulled out a ring box.

"I wanted to do this more privately, but since we've got a moment now where we're not fighting or having a crisis, I wanted to ask you to be my wife." Chase offered her the ring. The rose gold band was shaped like a cage and covered with diamonds. Inside the cage were platinum links that resembled chains. Each link had a black diamond on it.

"I've never seen anything like it," she whispered, sliding it on and admiring it. Marrying again hadn't been on the agenda, but Colleen realized that it was the only way they would be able to be together for the long term. He was too insecure without the bond of marriage to trust that her job wouldn't tempt her away from him. And she liked that this meant he was invested in their relationship, even though his temper overruled his common sense most of the time.

"It's unique. Just like you. I had it made for you after our first night together in your office. I knew then that I've never stopped loving you."

Colleen cupped his cheek, her heart melting at the utter devotion she saw in his eyes. "Chase."

He barely stood up in time as she came crashing into his arms. "I love you, too. I always have." This time it would be different. They would always fight. They were both used to having their own way. But now they would be joined together—if not by the true bond of mistress and submissive, than by marriage.

"You know what this means?" he said, cradling her close.

"What?" Colleen's reply was muffled against his shirt.

"We can get as pissed off as we want and storm out.

Because now we'll know we'll have something to come back to when things calm down."

She lifted her head up. "I still reserve the right to throw your clothes out a window and slap you silly."

"Only if you make it up to me afterward, Mistress."

Colleen kissed him until a nurse harrumphed behind them.

"Ms. Desmond would like you to escort Mr. Olenev out of her room."

"Were those her exact words?" Colleen asked over her shoulder.

"No. I don't use that kind of language," the nurse said primly.

"I think I'm going to need your help," Colleen said to Chase.

"I got your back, babe." Chase kissed her. "Always."

The End

COMING SOON!

BOOK FOUR IN THE CLUB INFERNO
SERIES!

Passion

New mom, Nefertiti "Tee" Robinson, wishes new dad Istvahn Olenev wanted to marry her because he loved her and couldn't bear to be parted. Instead, she's pretty sure he wants to put a ring on her finger because he knocked her up and wants their son to have both parents in his life. It's not that she disagrees, but she is a modern woman who doesn't need a husband. Since they both live and work at Couture -- a fashion resort that fronts a secret sex club, it's not as if he's not going to see little Khai every day anyway.

It's hard to resist him when she sees father and son together. Tee knows that marriages have been based on worse beginnings, but she's not ready to give up on having someone love her without all the baggage that Istvahn and she have. The first eight months of Khai's life is a lot of adjusting and Tee is too tired and scattered to concentrate on a romance anyway.

But when Istvahn arranges for their boss Colleen and her

new husband Chase to watch the baby for a long weekend, she jumps at the chance to sleep late and find herself again. Since they're not leaving Couture, if anything goes wrong or if she missing Khai, Tee can just go up a few flights of stairs. But she hadn't expected Istvahn to be sharing this mini vacation with her. He's set up dungeon scenes that rivals most of the kinky productions she's seen during her time as Colleen's administrative assistant. Suddenly, the handsome enigmatic head of security that she's dallied with a few times is this Russian lover of such intensity, she fears for her heart and her sanity.

Book Five: Desire – Dante's story
Coming soon by popular demand.

Want to be the first to find out when Passion & Desire releases or maybe get an early review copy? Find out how, here: http://jamiekschmidt.weebly.com/newsletter.

romance)

Necessary Evil

Sentinel's Kiss

Warden's Woman (***coming soon..***)

Ryder's Dream (***coming soon..***)

Stand-alone novels (high heat contemporary romance)

2018 Rita® Finalist in Erotic Romance:

Stud Hard Cover

Spice -

*Book Three in the Fate Series - Co-written with **Jenna Jameson***

Maiden Voyage

Stand-alone Novels & Novellas

Trinity (erotic ménage paranormal romance)

Midnight Lady, A Bad Girls book (high heat fantasy romance)

Naked Truth (romantic suspense)

Santa Genie (erotic paranormal romance)

Samurai's Heart (erotic paranormal romance)

A Casual Christmas (contemporary romance)

Betrayed (erotic paranormal romance)

Anthologies & Collections

Graveyard Shift (High heat paranormal romance)

Flash Magic (No heat at all speculative fiction stories)

ABOUT THE AUTHOR

USA Today bestselling author, Jamie K. Schmidt, writes erotic contemporary love stories and paranormal romances. Her steamy, romantic comedy, Life's a Beach, reached #65 on USA Today, #2 on Barnes & Noble and #9 on Amazon and iBooks. Her Club Inferno series has hit both the Amazon and Barnes & Noble top one hundred lists. The first book in the series, Heat, put her on the USA Today bestseller list for the first time, and is a #1 Amazon bestseller. Her book Stud is a 2018 Romance Writers of America Rita® Finalist in Erotica. Her dragon paranormal romance series has been called "fun and quirky" and "endearing." Partnered with New York Times bestselling author and former porn actress, Jenna Jameson, Jamie's hardcover debut, SPICE, continues Jenna's FATE trilogy.

Jamie's links:

Facebook URL
www.facebook.com/jamie.k.schmidt.1

Twitter URL
https://twitter.com/Jamiekswriter

Goodreads URL
http://www.goodreads.com/jamiekswriter

Website URL
http://jamiekschmidt.weebly.com/

Blog URL
http://jamiekswriter.livejournal.com/

Amazon Author Page
http://www.amazon.com/Jamie-K.-Schmidt/e/B00B7CKKO6

Pinterest
http://pinterest.com/jamiekswriter/